Praise for K.G. Anderson

"My favorites of the lot are K.G. Anderson's 'The Right Man for the Job' in which frustrated Democrats hold a séance in an attempt to find a solution to our Trump problem. It's witty and fun!"

— review of *More Alternative Truths* at Amazon.com

"'Patti 209,' by K.G. Anderson, is a sad story—and one that may stick with you a while. Like its predecessor, it's written—and well written, too—from an 'if this goes on' perspective."

— review of *Alternative Truths* at AmazingStories.com

"The chilling 'Politics as Usual' by K.G. Anderson hit close to home for me, as I often drive past the Pittsburgh Synagogue used as a backdrop for this story. Interestingly, this is not for a debate about gun control, but rather a cleverly woven timetable that illustrates how voter suppression might evolve."

— review of *Alternative Truths: Endgame* on Amazon.com

"K.G. Anderson's first-person account of living in Seattle after Trump declares it a terrorist zone, 'Unwanted Visitors,' is harrowing. The 'Good Germans' aspect of the story even more so."

— review of *Alternative Liberties* on Amazon.com

Patti 209

Fifteen Tales of the Very Near Future

K.G. Anderson

UnCommon Sense • Seattle

Cover Illustration: Rawpixel.com

Cover Design: Clarissa C. S. Ryan

Published in the United States by Uncommon Sense

Issued in print and electronic formats

Ebook ISBN 978-1-967682-00-3

Paperback ISBN 978-1-967682-01-0

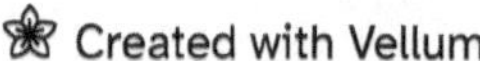 Created with Vellum

This book is dedicated to the memory of my father,
Lowell O. Anderson, who raised me on Herblock political
cartoons and took me to hear Shirley Chisholm speak
during her 1972 presidential campaign.

Contents

Foreword

It's said that Bob Brown's B Cubed Press invented the subgenre of Political Horror, beginning with the anthology *Alternative Truths* in 2017. So it's no surprise that quite a few of the tales in this collection first appeared in B Cubed Press anthologies.

At the times that I wrote them, I assumed most of these stories—wild exaggerations of bizarre proposals from the American Right—would be quickly outdated.

But, no. Exactly the opposite has happened: From absurd to horrific, nearly all of the predictions in these stories have come true—most of them in the first months of 2025.

In 2017, in "The Right Man for the Job," I summoned the ghost of President Lyndon B. Johnson. Visited in the afterlife by the spirits of journalist Molly Ivins, politician Adlai Stevenson II, and CBS news anchor Walter

Cronkite, LBJ learns that the landmark achievements of his 1960s Great Society are in grave danger:

> The former president, who'd leaned down to pet one of his two beagles, straightened up and peered at them over his wire-rim glasses. As his guests exchanged nervous glances, his smile slowly faded. "Oh, hell. It's Trump, isn't it?"
>
> The three nodded.
>
> "Well what's he destroyed now? School lunches? Public education? Equal opportunity? Head Start? Medicare? Social Security?"
>
> "Pretty much all of it," Ivins said. "Plus healthcare, foreign relations, and the environment."
>
> "What the hell is left?" Johnson shouted. "What happened to the Great Society? What happened to the United States?"

What, indeed? Today, many of us are asking that same question. *What happened to the United States?*

While the tales in this collection describe deeply troubled times, the characters in them model resistance, in many forms and at many costs. It's my hope that these stories will provoke thought, fuel discussion, and provide inspiration.

—K.G. Anderson

May 2025

Introduction

Everyone can imagine the perfect lunch. For each of us, it would be different.

My perfect lunch would be one where the food is good, the mood joyous, and the company perfect. It would be at the Kennedy Center's rededication, at a time when the current madness has been pushed into history.

It would, of course, be at the Rooftop Terrace Restaurant; I would have the salmon salad. It would be a table for four. I would wear my hearing aids because I wouldn't want to miss a word spoken at the event.

At this perfect lunch, the guests would be iconic visionaries with incredible insights into humanity and the ability to express them.

There would be Alice Walker—you may know her for her Pulitzer Prize winning novel, *The Color Purple*. I came to know her from a quote I read. She said, "The most common way people lose their power is by thinking they don't have any." This is truth in its most unadulterated form.

From beyond the grave there would be Molly Ivins. A woman who lived a life that any journalist would envy, with a sharp pen, a savage wit, and a humble soul. I was introduced to Molly Ivins' work by the author of this book —a woman whose presence at the table would complete it, and make memories for a lifetime. That is K.G. Anderson, the woman whose stories you are about to read.

She has the wit of Molly Ivins, the talent of Alice Walker, and a tenacity that I believe is all her own. She is unmatched in her ability to present life in the context of the political background. The politics are there, but the story comes first.

In this book, you will read stories of humor, tragedy, love and loss. But you will read them because once begun, a story by K.G. Anderson will capture your soul. She is a brilliant writer and this book will stay with you as few collections ever will.

Congratulations to you for making such a brilliant selection—and remember to write a review.

As for me? I've got to go now, the perfect lunch waits for me, if only in my imagination.

Be well.

—Bob Brown
March 2025

Patti 209

The alarms went off at midnight, up and down the hall of the nursing home: beeps, chimes, clicks, and snippets of golden oldies circa 2023. God, I still loathed Taylor Swift.

"It's twelve A.M.," an electronic voice informed my fellow inmates.

I heard the racket even through the locked door of the bathing room where I sat in the scratched-up fiberglass tub reading an old paperback mystery. Someone had complained last week that I used too much hot water.

"It would be appreciated if you would try drinking a hot beverage instead," read the reprimand I received. It was signed "Charming Devreaux, Care Manager."

That Devreaux bitch wouldn't know Care if it bit her, but she certainly knew how to Manage. She tracked every bite of food, every washcloth, and every toothbrush—to say nothing of every bandage, battery, adult diaper, and pill. And she kept an eagle eye on the staff. Employees who wasted time giving Care were replaced by less expensive, more tractable people. The underpaid caregivers we wound up with were a far cry from the skilled professionals and intelligent robots I'd imagined forty years ago when I was designing the Fiddler's Green Retirement Community. Robots? Hah!

All right, so the prices of everything, from utilities to medical services, had soared beyond our original estimates. But it was envy that led one of my fellow inmates to rat me out for excessive bathing. I was the only one of us still limber enough to get in and out of the tub without help. Thanks to the yoga regimen I'd started at 50 and adhered to grimly for thirty-five years, old Patti 209 was still a moving target.

I stood up carefully, grasped the grab bar, and stepped out onto the threadbare non-slip mat. I toweled dry then wrapped myself in a worn blue cotton robe. It had been labeled with black laundry marker, front and back: *Patti 209.*

Yep, that's me. I grimaced at my reflection in the chipped bathroom mirror: a mop of wiry white hair, a wrinkled face, and dark, glinting eyes. A little old lady. But not a nice one.

I padded quietly down the wide, dim-lit hallway to my room—not that anyone would hear me. Our lone night aide was downstairs at his desk in the first-floor office, earbuds in, snoring away. An hour ago he'd failed to respond to the muffled crashes from the common room where my husband, Danny, was having another bad night—pacing back and forth, cursing, and upending furniture. Those gene-targeting dementia treatments I'd spent a fortune on for him weren't having much effect.

Through a half-open door I glimpsed our newest inmate —Tod? Or was it Ted?—slumped at his desk in front of a laptop. He had his pants unzipped and a porn vid running. Ragged snores came from Chuck Olsen's room, where a battered black mobi was parked by the bed.

In the next room a series of soft beeps indicated a vital-signs monitor sending cardiac data to some devicemaker's network. How reassuring. Except we'd found out last month, when Kamala Pasil died in her sleep, that there were no longer people at the other end of the line reviewing those data transmissions. Though the company kept sending us the bills.

Beep. Beep.

I knocked on Rachel's door.

"Come in." Rachel sat in her faded wing chair holding one of those stupid robotic Petsies on her lap. A dog, I guessed. Rachel has macular degeneration and the Petsy's glowing green eyes, connected to her brain by an implant, give her a kind of vision.

"Agent 209, sneaking back from clandestine bathing activities," I announced as I entered. We giggled. Then a crash from downstairs sobered us.

"Danny's having another bad night," she said.

I didn't answer, but sat down on the bench beside her chair. I was glad she couldn't see my face. Just the mention of my husband's name and I felt like I'd been punched in the stomach.

"Not how we pictured things, is it?" Rachel went on. "What did that stupid magazine article call Fiddler's Green—'the new old-age lifestyle?' "

I snorted. "Yeah. For us old New-Agers."

Thirty-five years ago Rachel and I had designed what we were confident would be an alternative to the cheerless nursing homes where we'd guiltily warehoused our own parents. Foundation grants poured in to our design collective. Conferences across the country lauded our work. In 2016 we'd opened Fiddler's Green, complete with solar power and universal access, gray water recycling, ergonomic design and lighting, workshops and gardens. Just add old people, and—

Another crash from downstairs, followed by a bellow of rage.

"Patti..." Rachel hesitated. "We all love him, but Danny can't go on like this. Not with the police."

Danny kept escaping. His new electronic tracking bracelet had taken the Fiddler's Green staff several days to figure out but Danny, with his engineering background, had disabled it in minutes. He kept wandering away and they kept calling the police to find him. Charming Devreaux said the next time it happened, he'd be kicked out of Fiddler's Green.

"Our nephew back East is furious," I told Rachel. "Special memory-care facilities are expensive. If I send Danny to one, it will eat up the money he thinks he'll inherit."

"So surprise the greedy nephew and leave your money to the treehuggers instead," Rachel said. "Are there any trees left these days?"

I chuckled. Sadly, giving away our money wasn't an option. Very little remained of the nest egg Danny and I had retired with twenty years ago, thanks to the repeal of Social Security and Medicare.

Now tens of thousands of us old farts—oh, excuse me, *the elderly*—lived in decaying houses, their utilities disconnected, or were homeless in camps and shelters. Danny and I were comparatively lucky, owning a founder's share in Fiddler's Green and praying the place could stay in business until—well, until the two of us were gone. There was talk of British Columbia annexing the Pacific Northwest, but we'd been hearing that since 2029, when Kushner's first act as president had been to sell what was left of Florida—including the impoverished residents—to Cuba.

"If I don't shell out for the memory-care place in Seattle, management is going to send Danny to a state facility."

Rachel gasped. We'd heard horror stories about these grim warehouses the government had set up for the poor devils who'd failed to respond to the generic Alzheimer's pill. "But you and Danny are founders here," she said. "Doesn't that count for something?"

I shook my head. "You'd think. But my attorney said it would take years to fight this. And the courts are barely functioning. Even if we won, it would be too late for Danny."

"Oh, Patti, you'll miss him." Rachel reached out and found my arm. She squeezed it.

"No," I said. "Wherever Danny does, I go with him. He's my husband—what's left of him. I can't just send him away, and—"

Rachel's stuffed robot gave a doggy little yip. Probably sick of my maundering.

"Damn. That means it's time for my pills." Rachel groped around on the table beside her.

I handed her the little plastic box with compartments coded in Braille.

"All I do these days is look for things I've lost," she said. "Or think I've lost something and end up wondering if I ever had it at all." She took a sip from a bottle of water and gulped a pill. "No wonder they gave us all numbers."

Numbers? Oh yes, the numbers. I didn't tell her I'd overheard Charming Devreaux on the phone with someone, asking about tattooing our numbers on our arms. "But it'll make it easier to keep track of them," she'd whined.

Number tattoos. At least the woman hadn't said anything about furnaces. Yet.

I gave Rachel a quick kiss goodnight and continued down the hall. Fiddler's Green. My life's work. I doubted a soul in the place except Rachel and the bookkeeper could remember my last name. Or knew that I was the architect who'd designed the place. Even Danny rarely recognized me, poor man.

I started down the flight of stairs (wide and securely banistered, but not very well lit these days—and what had become of the motion sensors?) to the ground floor kitchen. I resisted the temptation to take the elevator, even though the argument with Danny's nephew this morning had worn me out. I'd have gone to bed right after my bath, but I'd have felt guilty. Because I wanted to make cocoa and toast for Sharelle.

Sharelle, my best friend for more than fifty years, was in the garden shed. In July she'd talked the housekeepers into moving her bed into the quaint, shingled cottage with its rudimentary half bath. It was a whim, Sharelle told us, deploying her Southern charm to deflect our concerns. How she enjoyed the summer nights in her garden, and there would be so few summers left...

Now the nights had turned cold, but Sharelle refused to come back in the main building except to take a shower or gobble a meal. I'd taken to luring her into the kitchen with a late-night snack. I'd found the codes for the locked refrigerator and cabinets and I'd bribed the night aides into looking the other way.

Sharelle and I would sit at the old Formica table one of the housekeepers had put in the kitchen and reminisce. Though the past few nights she'd responded to my remarks with nonsensical phrases, wolfing her toast as if she thought someone were going to snatch it. I tried to ignore the way she used the hem of her baggy sweatshirt as a napkin and let her long gray dreadlocks trail in her food.

Minetta, the newest housekeeper, was under orders from Charming to get Sharelle back inside. She'd enlisted my help, but when we went out to the cottage Sharelle just shook her head and curled up on the rug, a Moroccan carpet brought from her old room.

"Patti, Sharelle's not in her right mind," was how Minetta put it after we'd retreated to the kitchen. She tapped one finger to her neatly coiffed head and pursed her lips.

"Yes. I know. I'll call her daughter."

"Will you? Really?"

"Soon."

"We have to move her inside by Friday. Charming says so."

We sighed. Minetta patted my hand, her touch so warm, and turned to unload the dishwasher.

To my surprise, Sharelle was not waiting for me in the kitchen tonight. It must be the rain. Peering out the window, I saw the cottage was dark. She'd probably fallen asleep.

I went ahead and made our cocoa, flavoring the drinks from a tiny bottle of vanilla I kept in the pocket of my robe. I loaded the cups onto a tray, covered the tray with plastic wrap to keep it dry, and headed cautiously out to the shed. We'd designed the back door to open level to the deck and pathway—no treacherous steps to contend with. That was fortunate, because in these days of short-staffing, the deck was untended and covered with slippery moss.

Oh, Rachel and I hadn't been completely stupid. We'd understood the house. We'd understood old people. We just hadn't quite grasped that the frail old people we were so tenderly designing it for would be us. Or that the country we lived in would wish we were dead.

When I entered the dark cottage the fragrance of potting soil and drying herbs rose up like fumes from an aged Scotch. No cleansers, no mopping solution, no stench of overcooked food and under-washed bodies. Couldn't blame Sharelle for making this place her refuge.

"Sharelle? Sharelle!" I slid the tray onto the table and felt around on the wall for the light switch. A soft glow from the single bulb fell on the table, revealing a delicate etched cordial glass with a few drops of red wine left at the bottom.

Sharelle lay on the bed in the corner.

"Sharelle? Honey?" I grabbed her hand.

It was limp and cold, the wrist without pulse. I put my face to her lips.

Sharelle wasn't breathing.

The world stopped and I found myself outside the reach of time. I had prepared myself to be old, but not to feel so utterly alone. I backed away and crumpled into a chair. *Old. Alone.* The words echoed.

When I emerged from my trance, Sharelle's body still lay there on the bed. Our cocoa still sat on the table. I slowly removed the plastic wrap from the tray, fumbling as tears blurred my vision. I raised one of the warm cups to my lips, toasted my friend, and drank. It was Dutch chocolate, mixed with sugar, heated in a pan with milk slowly added, taken from the burner when it was just hot enough, and kissed with a few drops of vanilla. The way my grandmother had made it, and my mother. I'd begun making it for Sharelle after she'd confided that our usual tea was keeping her awake at night.

Oh, Sharelle! I closed my eyes, and suddenly recalled Sharelle this summer, tucking a bottle of pills into an antique copper vase. I'd held the chair steady while she climbed onto it and set the vase on a high shelf above the table. The vase held a prescription bottle with our secret stash of pills—opiates that should have been doled out under the watchful eye of a nurse.

Well, someone hadn't been so watchful.

I opened my eyes and looked up. Yes, the vase was gone from the shelf. Now it stood on Sharelle's bedside table. I turned it over and dumped out the contents. The bottle was there, but a third of the pills were gone. There was a note penned on a scrap of paper in a faltering script.

"Patti, it was time. Saved plenty for you, girl. Love, Sharelle."

I tucked the bottle of pills and the incriminating note into a pocket of my robe. I was shivering. *What to do next?* I wished I weren't so tired. I wished the cottage were warmer. I wished my hips didn't hurt like hell from the cold.

Outside the window, the porch light twinkled like a beacon in the mist, calling me back to the house. I started across. Forgetting the moss on the deck, I slid, lost my balance, then caught myself on the handrail. I stood there, panting with fear and for a second my imagination saw me going down hard, hitting my head, then sprawled out as still as Sharelle. For a second I thought, *Then someone else can deal with this shit.*

It passed. I staggered to the door, and the keypad recognized my palm. I stepped inside the building to find…silence. I frowned. Was Danny gone? Or just sleeping?

Exhaustion swept over me. There was nothing I could do. Suddenly the stairs up to our room seemed insurmountable. Like the old lady I now knew I was, I rode the goddamn elevator up to our room on the second floor.

As I reached the door of the room and grasped the handle, I heard a musical chime. And another.

Someone's alarm, no doubt. Pushing open the door, I started.

Danny had found his guitar.

Months ago, afraid he'd smash it in one of his rages, I'd hidden the vintage Martin D-28 in the depths of our closet. Now my husband sat hunched on a chair, twisting the tuning pegs. His iron-grey hair was so crudely trimmed it hurt me to look at him. The skin on his jaw hung loose, covered in stubble.

I cringed as he clawed out a few discordant notes. Then his hands found a tune and he began whispering the words to that old song. Something about a road, a highway, between the dawn and the dark of night.

I don't think he'd played that one in 30 years. Or maybe he had and I hadn't been listening.

When the last note of the song faded, I smeared a tear across my cheek with the heel of my hand and brought my palms together in soft applause. Danny, his hands trembling, tried to set the guitar against the wall. It started to slide, and I caught it. I set it safe in the corner. Then I looked over to see Danny, his head buried in his big, tired hands. He might have been crying.

I made my way back down the stairs to the kitchen to mix up another pot of cocoa. As the mixture grew warm and fragrant, I followed the smell back to a sunny morning when I'd stood at the stove in my grandmother's kitchen with my whole life in front of me.

I'd imagined travels, a husband, a family, singing, dancing...I'd never imagined I'd end up as Patti 209.

The digital clock on the stove read 3 a.m. Outside the window, rain battered the blackness. Just a few hours until the day staff arrived. When the cocoa was hot I took two mugs from the cabinet and poured from the pan. I reached into the pocket of my robe, fumbling not for the vanilla but for Sharelle's pills.

A hand grabbed my arm. I turned to see Danny looking down at me with sad eyes. I don't know if he recognized me, but he recognized something. He dropped his hunched shoulders and shuffled closer to give me the first hug I'd had from anyone in a long, long time.

"Danny," I said. "Danny."

There was no response.

When his arms fell away, I turned back to the cocoa. He watched as I put our cups on a tray and he shuffled along behind me as I carried it out to the common room. We sat on the sofa. I drew out the bottle of pills.

At the sight of them, he growled. I struggled with the plastic cap. He waved me, and the bottle, away. I poured half of the pills into my hand.

"It's the last time you'll ever have to take them, darling," I said, my voice high and sweet and barely my own. "Twenty of them. Can you count them?"

Danny grunted and picked a pill from my hand.

"One," I said.

He took a second pill.

"Two. Very good! After the pills, you can have some cocoa."

Danny still loved counting, and with my coaching, made his way through all twenty. Then he gulped some cocoa and set down his mug on the edge of the tray, where it tumbled onto the rug. By the time I'd mopped up the mess, he was busy pulling books from one of the bookcases and piling them on the floor. In the kitchen I cleaned up all evidence of our poisonous picnic, loaded the pot and the dishes into the dishwasher, turned it on, and put away the tray. When I came out, Danny was kneeling on the floor in the common room, tearing pages out of a book and humming.

I rode the elevator back upstairs, crawled into bed, and cried myself to sleep.

* * *

The crash of the bookcase didn't wake me. What did was Charming Devreaux, shaking my shoulder. What the hell was the bitch doing in our room?

"Patti," she said.

I batted away her hand and sat up in bed. A stocky young woman stood in the doorway. A woman in the dark blue uniform of an EMT.

"Come with us, please," Charming said. Her voice was trembling. The events of the previous night were coming back to me and I wondered which one of them she'd discovered. Danny? Sharelle?

Tying the sash on my robe and raking my fingers through my hair, I followed Charming and the EMT to the stairs. On the way down I caught a glimpse of another EMT and one of our aides as they wheeled a bulky body on a stretcher out the front door.

"Danny!" I stopped at the foot of the stairs and turned to Charming. She nodded. I felt relief, then embarrassment to be standing there in my robe.

"I'll go get dressed," I mumbled. I thought of black trousers, a black sweater, and a silver-and-turquoise pin, a gift from Danny, that would be right for the occasion.

"Patti," Charming said, her voice surprisingly kind. "He's dead. He must have had a...a stroke. The bookcase fell...a head injury. There was nothing anyone could do."

Her hand on my shoulder was trembling. *She has a heart after all*, I thought. Then I realized: *Lawsuit. The bitch is afraid I'll sue. She has no idea what really happened.*

"A stroke?" I stuttered convincingly. I nodded my stunned agreement. Blank I could do. Blank was so easy.

The EMT was watching me. A dark-skinned, short-haired woman with the build of a cop, she bore the green and black tracings of a cybernetic information system on her cheek below her eye. I'd heard the EMTs were part of law enforcement now.

"I am very sorry," the EMT said in a soft, melodic voice. It held a trace of an accent I could not place. "Danny Richmond was a hero of mine. I own all his recordings. I have tried for years to play in his style. Your husband was a great artist, ma'am."

Charming's look of astonishment pleased me no end.

"Wait!" I beckoned the EMT, who'd turned to leave the building. "Wait! Please! I have something I'd like to give you."

She followed me back upstairs to our room, where I placed Danny's guitar into its case and handed it to her. She thanked me again and again.

After she left, I took my time dressing. I carefully transferred Sharelle's pills from my bathrobe into the pocket of the sweater I wore. I'd keep them on me until I found a good hiding place.

By the time I got down to the dining room, an aide had discovered Sharelle's body out in the shed. As I spooned my oatmeal, I listened to a man at the next table speculate about what new inmates Charming would admit to replace Sharelle and Danny.

"They'll be able to pay full price, you can bet on that," someone whispered, triggering a ripple of nervous laughter.

I felt a shaky hand on my shoulder. Tod—or was it Ted?—murmured, "I'm very sorry about Danny. And about Sharelle."

I nodded and closed my lips over another spoonful of warm, mushy oats.

When it was time to go back upstairs I hesitated at the door of my room. Danny and his guitar were gone. But they were both safe now.

And, thanks to Sharelle, Patti 209 could still take care of herself. I patted the pocket of my sweater and felt the bottle of pills.

A bath tonight would be good. I'd use all the goddamn hot water I wanted.

Everything Is Fixed Now

Derek Tye, the DataNex sys op, glanced up to see Liz Ferry standing at the entrance of his cluttered cubicle. Tall, slim, wearing her signature outfit of crisp white blouse, black pants, and four-inch high heels, she'd come armed with a legal pad. Derek returned his attention to the tests running on his screen.

Liz cleared her throat loudly. Then spoke his name.

"Busy," he said.

"Those emails we discussed...?"

Derek shrugged his massive shoulders. "Yeah."

"Those emails are gone?"

He swiveled slowly in his chair to regard her. "Yeah. Done." He swiveled back.

"From everywhere?" she said. "I mean, aren't there backups?"

"Erased." He said. "Out of the system."

The *snick, snick, snick* of her high heels on the carpeting told him he'd seen the last of her.

The emails were indeed gone from the DataNex company system. They existed only on the thumb drive Derek had taken home with him. Just in case.

* * *

Email to Dawayne Johnson, Manager, Quality Assurance from: Liz Ferry, Manager, Vibrante Fitness—Subject: Limit QA scope on Vibrante

Hey—Engineering's getting out-of-scope questions from someone on your team about the Vibrante data.

Reminder: your team is supposed to be looking for issues with ease-of-use and accuracy for the Vibrante device personal fitness features (steps, heartbeat, weight). I understand there may have been confusion because of the additional data fields coming in.

Just ignore those. That additional data is being QA-d by the third-party, overseas group.

BTW it wouldn't hurt to remind everyone of their non-disclosure agreements.

Email to Samantha Cook, Quality Assurance from Dawayne Johnson—Subject: Request from Liz Ferry

Take a look at the email from Liz I just forwarded. She says just ignore that "extra" data. It's nothing we need to be looking at.

Please check with me in the future before sending any questions to Engineering.

Email to Dawayne Johnson from Samantha Cook— Subject: Re: Request from Liz Ferry

Did you know the extra data is medical data? Heartbeat patterns, respiration, pulse measurements, etc. So are we going to market the Vibrante as a medical device after the FDA oversight is phased out in 2019?!?

I contacted Engineering because the heartbeat data was in an alert zone for three users in Comette's employee fitness incentive program. Engineering said not to worry, but I did some digging and it looks as through these three people are experiencing periods of ventricular tachycardia. (My sister died of sudden cardiac arrest playing softball in high school. We found out later that she had undiagnosed heart problems and probably had ventricular tachycardia before she went into sudden cardiac arrest.)

Liz's group REALLY needs to contact the companies who have those employees in the Vibrante program and advise them to get them to a cardiologist (a regular medical exam WON'T detect this type of problem). Also, to have them STOP doing the Vibrante fitness program.

Email to Samantha Cook from Dawayne Johson— Subject: Re: Re: Request from Liz Ferry

Thanks for that info. I'll pass your message up to Liz's team just in case they haven't already gotten it from the QA contractors.

Email to Dawayne Johnson from Samantha Cook— Subject: Re: Re: Re: Request from Liz Ferry

Give the Liz the IDs for the users with the cardiac data issues:

5-2889 (female, 49, Comette group)

8-3445 (male, 24, Lumar Electric group)

8-0871 (male, 45, Cebardok group)

The first two are assigned to a 3x/week, high-intensity cardio program--very scary!

Email to Liz Ferry from Dawayne Johnson—Subject: User data—3 alerts

Samantha Cook says she's spotted a big problem with three of the employee fitness program participants. I'm sure you've already had this reported by the outside QA group, but just FYI.

What with medical data, employee confidentiality, that sort of thing this is probably a little tricky. Obviously, I'm not sure what agreements we have in place with the participants or their companies.

Email to Dawayne Johnson from Liz Ferry—Subject: Re: User date—3 alerts

Not to worry. Our QA contractor has spotted that data and we're handling it. All taken care of.

Reminder: No member of your team is authorized to contact any individual user, or any representative of the customer companies that are implementing the Vibrante program with their employees.

Sticky note left on Dawayne Johnson's desk by Samantha Cook:

5-2889 IS STILL DOING THE CARDIO. ANOTHER EPISODE OF V. TACHYCARDIA. CAN WE CONTACT THIS WOMAN DIRECTLY? NEED NAME, CONTACT INFO.

Email to Samantha Cook from Dawayne Johnson— Subject: Short meeting

Stop by my office after lunch and I'll brief you on a new project. I think you'll like it more than the Vibrante work.

Text Message to Samantha Cook from Dawayne Johnson, 9:07 a.m.

Hey, you OK? We missed you at this morning's meeting

Text Message to Dawayne Johnson from Liz Ferry, 9:19 a.m.

Just got a call from the director of HR at Comette. She was approached outside their company fitness facility this morning by a young woman who saw her wearing a Vibrante device and then asked "some odd questions" about her health. She said the young woman approached four other women wearing the Vibrante.

Call me IMMEDIATELY.

Text Message to Samantha Cook from Dawayne Johnson, 9:21 a.m.

Urgent. PHONE me.

Email to Samantha Cook from Marcus Jiang-Hewitt, Director, Human Resources—Subject: Your probation

Your six-week probation commences today. During this time, your attendance and performance will be monitored and feedback provided by your manager on a weekly basis.

In addition, you are advised to meet with a counselor from one of the third-party agencies available to DataNex employees. A list is attached. Please contact me or a member of the HR staff with any questions.

Email to Samantha Cook from Dawayne Johnson, copied to Prisha Joshi, Simplex-Tone—Subject: New assignment with Simplex-Tone

Starting Monday, you'll be doing QA for Prisha Joshi's team on the Simplix-Tone. They've got a desk set up for you in L Building. I think you'll enjoy working with them.

I'll send you meeting requests for the follow-ups HR wants.

Email to Samantha Cook from Dawayne Johnson— Subject: Good news

Just met with Liz Ferry. The users you were concerned about have been removed from the Vibrante program. Thought you'd want to know. All good!

Hope you're enjoying the work on Simplix-Tone. Looking forward to hearing about it at our Thursday check-in.

Email to Dawayne Johnson from Samantha Cook— Subject: Re: Good news

>>Removed from the Vibrante program

No! Lily Pang was also removed from her JOB. I tracked her down. When Comette let her go, they didn't tell her anything about her heart problem, or advise her to see a cardiologist. They just mysteriously "eliminated" her job.

And she was the lucky one. Mark Richardson? The 24-year-old guy from Lumar Electric? He's been "removed" too -- because he went into sudden cardiac arrest and DIED.

The people at Comette are using our data to find employees at risk for heart problems -- maybe other health problems -- and fire them! Does Liz's team have any idea?

Email to Liz Ferry from P. Ellis Nevars, Corporate Counsel—Subject: Changes at OSHA

You are correct. The federal Occupational Safety and Health Administration's mandate to investigate corporate whistleblower-retaliation complaints (The Whistleblower Protection Act of

1989, Pub.L. 101-12 as amended) was largely eliminated as of March 15. There was an exception for the transportation industry.

We have already briefed HR and Security about the implications for DataNex, but I appreciate your checking with me to confirm. Please let me know if you require any additional information.

Email to Luther Beckshire, CEO, DataNex, from Liz Ferry. Subject: Vibrante Next Steps

Everything is fixed now.

Security conducted the exit interviews with the two former employees yesterday evening. We are confident that they will not be sharing any proprietary information about our products with outside organizations. There had been an attempt to send screenshots from a company laptop to an external server, but Security anticipated and dealt with that breach.

Sales met last week with two Fortune 500 companies and one government agency interested in the Vibrante program for large, multi-site employee groups. All three are ready to begin using our enhanced data capabilities for HR purposes as soon as the FDA is out of the picture next month.

Two of the prospects also asked about obtaining data on employee galvanic skin responses for use by their internal security teams. Can you remind Gil and Engineering to fast-track those sensor features for the Q4 rollout? Marketing is working up a GSR pricing model that dovetails with sales goals. Details at tomorrow's meeting.

The Right Man for
the Job

The chief of staff for a U.S. senator paused in the kitchen doorway, a bottle of chilled Sauterne in each hand. "I can't believe we've come to this," he said.

His wife, a political advisor to the 2016 Clinton campaign, pulled trays of desserts out of the stainless steel refrigerator. "You mean Trump?"

"No!" With a jerk of his head, he indicated the formal dining room down the hall of their Silver Spring home. "I mean a séance. *Really*?"

His wife, her features drawn with stress and exhaustion, shrugged. "Why the hell not?" she asked. "People keep saying 'If only Molly Ivins were here! If only Walter Cronkite could see this!' So I figured, why not? We'll call them back to help us!"

"But...a séance?" her husband said.

"You have a better idea?"

He shrugged. Together they entered the dimly lit dining room and joined the ten high-ranking Democrats seated around the damask-draped oval table. Conversation stopped when a middle-aged woman in an evening gown, shawl, and black silk turban appeared in the opposite doorway. She took the chair at the head of the table and extended her be-ringed hands to the guests on either side of her.

"Turn off ze lights," she said. "And ve shall begin."

The host, seated at the foot of the table, leaned over and whispered to his wife. "Nice touch, the Eastern European accent. I hope she's not a friend of—."

"Shut up, dear," his wife hissed. She clasped his hand, somewhat more tightly than necessary, and the séance began.

* * *

The bright yellow river raft bumped the dock, and a sturdy woman clambered out. She wore jeans, a chambray shirt, and a down vest. Her reddish-blonde hair was tied back in a ponytail. She waved enthusiastically to the dapper, balding man sitting at a table on the front porch of the rustic lodge.

"Hiya, Adlai," she called as she strode up the lawn.

"Hello, Molly." He folded the copy of the *Washington Post* he'd been reading and rose to give her a peck on the cheek.

"You get the call from that séance?" She flopped down in a chair across from him and raised an eyebrow. She had a wide grin, sparkling blue eyes, and a Texas twang.

"Oh, yes. They must be getting desperate."

She nodded. "Apparently it's desperate times back there."

"Coffee?" he asked her. He looked back toward the open door into the lodge.

"I'd take a beer."

Seconds later a tall waiter appeared with a pot of coffee for Adlai Stevenson II and a chilled brown bottle of Lone Star for his guest. "Good to see you again, Miss Ivins."

She waved away an offered glass and took a long pull from the bottle. "Pretty soft here in the afterlife, isn't it?"

"Delightful," he said. "And so you know, I haven't the slightest desire to go back and help what currently passes for the Democratic Party deal with this Trump idiot. As my father said when he served as vice president, 'Your public servants serve you right.'"

Ivins grinned. Then she leaned forward, face serious. "Never met this Trump guy, didya?"

"Thank heavens, no. I left politics in 1965."

"Trump isn't really in politics," Ivins wrinkled her nose. "He's more of a celebrity. Had a TV show. It was all about him bullying people and then firing them. "

"Charming. I guess that's what it takes to get elected these days."

Ivins sipped her beer, squinting out at the river. It looked a lot like the Colorado but wasn't, really. "I missed the boat on Trump, you know. Had him in my sights. It was the run-up to the 2000 election and I joked, in the *Texas Observer*, about him 'being treated as though any reasonable citizen would consider voting for him.' Adlai, I *joked* about that. And look what happened. Boy, was I wrong about Trump."

Stevenson shrugged. "I'd say you were right about Trump but unduly optimistic about the American voter."

"I don't know." She gave a deep sigh. "It is the stories we don't get, the ones we miss, pass over, fail to recognize, don't pick up on, that will send us to hell."

Stevenson gestured to their pleasant surroundings. "This is hardly hell. Unless you've been rafting on the River Styx."

"Point taken," Ivins said, grinning. "But apparently they've now got hell back where we came from."

"Wasn't it always hell," he said, "somewhere?"

The phone in the lobby of the hotel rang and the tall waiter appeared in the doorway. "They're calling from that séance again. What should I tell them?"

"Oh, lord, don't tell them I'm here," Ivins said. "There's no way I'm going back. I wrote hundred of columns, dozens of books, and obviously nobody listened. What about you, Adlai? You going back?"

Stevenson waved away the waiter. "Not me. Not again. I made three runs for president, you know. I'll always remember that poor woman who assured me that I 'had the vote of every thinking American.'"

Ivins hooted. "As the story goes, you told her it would take a lot more than that."

Stevenson peered into his empty coffee cup. "These days, it might take an act of God."

"Speaking of which, you think we should get in touch with Walter?"

"Why not?" Stevenson brightened. "It would be good to see him again." He went into the lodge and took a London Fog raincoat and a fedora from the coat tree. Ivins kicked some of the dirt off her hiking books and hid a smile as he shrugged into his coat. For Adlai Stevenson II it would always be 1965.

The pair followed a plush maroon carpet runner into the depths of the lodge to a door rimmed with glowing blue lights.

"Gotta love these portals," Ivins said.

The door slid open. The pair stepped into what looked like an elevator and chanted in unison, "Walter Cronkite." Seconds later the chamber's doors opened into what looked like a comfortably appointed old Georgetown home, but wasn't, really. A mahogany door stood ajar. Stevenson knocked.

"Come in." The hearty voice would have been familiar to the millions who'd listened to CBS News in the 1960s and 70s.

Walter Cronkite, dressed in a blue blazer and dark trousers, came out from behind a nondescript gray desk and shook their hands, greeting each of them by first name. He motioned them to the comfortable leather office chairs in front of his desk and went back to his chair. "Well, what can I do for you two?"

Ivins and Stevenson exchanged surprised looks.

"Haven't you been getting calls from a spiritualist conducting a séance for a bunch of desperate Democrats?" Ivins asked.

"A séance?" The newsman gave an avuncular chuckle. "Afraid I'm out of the loop these days. Want to fill me in?"

"Adlai and I have been summoned by a spiritualist hired by the Democrats to bring some of us out of retirement to do something about Donald Trump."

"Trump!" Cronkite bellowed. His jowly face turned red. "Donald Trump! He ruined my neighborhood in Manhattan when he built that garish monstrosity of a tower. The man is an utter scoundrel."

"No argument here," Ivins said. "But keep in mind: you couldn't stop him building that tower, and the

Republicans couldn't stop him taking over their party, and the Democrats, bless their divisive little souls, couldn't stop him from taking the presidential election. And now that he's in office even his own Secretary of State can't stop him from trying to destroy the planet."

"Are you two going back to help?" Cronkite asked.

"Nope," said Ivins. "As far as I'm concerned, we gave it our best. And what could I do? There's certainly no shortage of pundits on the case."

Stevenson spoke up. "Walter, we were hoping that you might be able to help us find someone who'd want to go back to straighten things out. Jack Kennedy? Tip O'Neill? Bella Abzug? Paul Wellstone? Maybe Martin Luther King?"

Cronkite leaned back in his chair. He steepled his fingers and peered down at them, lost in thought. A small, tight, grin came to his face.

"You have an idea?" Ivins asked.

"As a matter of fact, Molly, I do. We need to pay a visit to the Ranch."

"The Ranch?" Stevenson shook his head. "I'm not really dressed for it. Maybe you two--"

"C'mon, Adlai." Ivins was grinning. "It's almost lunchtime and Lady Bird serves a mean chili."

"Johnson irritates me." Stevenson sighed as they followed Cronkite into the hallway. "I was his

Ambassador to the United Nations and, frankly, I don't think he listened to a word I said."

The trio entered the portal and chorused "LBJ."

"The old sumbitch," Ivins added. The portal didn't seem to mind.

* * *

The portal at the LBJ ranch turned out to be at the front gates, and the gates were a good five miles down the road from the ranch house. But as soon as the trio emerged from the portal they saw the rising dust cloud as a white Lincoln convertible came speeding down the driveway. It pulled up at the gate, and a grinning Lyndon B. Johnson got out and shook their hands.

"Good to see ya'll," he said. "Climb on in. We're just getting ready to sit down to some of Lady Bird's Pedernales River chili."

Steering with one hand, holding a plastic cup filled with Scotch in the other, Johnson regaled his visitors with tales of fishing and hunting all the way to the big ranch house. He didn't ask them what they'd come for until everyone had eaten at least two bowls of chili with cornbread and had insisted they couldn't possibly eat thirds.

Lady Bird brought in a pot of coffee for Stevenson and herself. Ivins was still drinking beer and both LBJ and Cronkite nursed tumblers of Scotch.

"I suppose we should get down to business," Johnson said. "It has to be business when you get a visit from a politician, a reporter, and a columnist." The former president, who'd leaned down to pet one of his two beagles, straightened up and peered at them over his wire-rim glasses. As his guests exchanged nervous glances, his smile slowly faded. "Oh, hell. It's Trump, isn't it?"

The three nodded.

"Well what's he destroyed now? School lunches? Public education? Equal opportunity? Head Start? Medicare? Social Security?"

"Pretty much all of it," Ivins said. "Plus healthcare, foreign relations, and the environment."

"What the hell is left?" Johnson shouted. "What happened to the Great Society? What happened to the United States?"

Under the table, a beagle howled.

"Lyndon," Lady Bird cautioned.

He shook her off. "Take it easy, Bird. I can't have a heart attack here, I'm already dead."

"And that is actually why we're here," Ivins said. "The Democratic party—what's left of it—is holding a séance and they're trying to summon one of us back from the dead to help them do something about Trump."

Johnson grinned a terrible grin. "I'd say you've found the right man for the job."

"Lyndon," his wife said.

He patted his mouth with a big linen napkin and stood up from the table. "Gotta make one call."

He gave Stevenson a meaningful glance.

"Your old neighbor?" Stevenson asked.

"Yessir," Johnson said. He headed down the hall and vanished into his library.

Lady Bird looked as annoyed as Cronkite had ever seen her.

"'Neighbor'?" asked Ivins.

Lady Bird took a deep breath. "J. Edgar Hoover. He was our neighbor back in the days when Lyndon was in Congress and we lived on 30th Place in Northwest D.C. I haven't spoken to that man after what he did to Walter Jenkins. But Lyndon...he never cuts a connection."

"Never know when they'll come in handy, Bird." It was Johnson again, sweeping through the dining room on his way to the front door. The beagles trotted behind him.

"Where are you going?" his wife called after him. She and Ivins ran into the hall.

"Back to the White House, of course." Johnson paused on the front porch, silhouetted against a rugged landscape that looked like Texas Hill Country but wasn't, really. "I'm not letting some asshole New York developer ruin all my hard work."

Everyone watched as LBJ put the dogs into the Lincoln and then vaulted into the driver's seat. Dust rose as he sped down the driveway toward the ranch's portal.

"What I'd give to see the look on the faces of those Democrats at the séance when he shows up," Stevenson said.

"They don't make Democrats like Lyndon anymore," Lady Bird said loyally.

"Hell, they don't even make *Texans* like that," Ivins said. She turned to Cronkite. "You want the last word, Walter?"

The news anchor nodded and lifted his glass. "And that's the way it is," he intoned.

"God help us," said Ivins.

* * *

"Fire them!" came the whiny, all-too-familiar voice from the Oval Office. "I'm the President of the United States. I demand that people around here do their jobs. Which means keeping the damned carpets clean."

The White House chief of staff stood in front of the president's desk, wringing his hands. "Mr. President, that was the fourth cleaning service. I can get a new one, but it will take several days just to get their security clearances."

"Fire the security people," came the answer. "Or I'll fire you! You're fired! You're fired! You're fired!"

The chief of staff turned and fled, stepping right into a fresh pile of dog shit on the burgundy carpet just outside of the Oval Office door. *Not again!* He hopped up and down on his other foot, bracing himself against the wall as he removed the smeared wingtip. From down the hallway and up the stairs, he distinctly heard the baying of...beagles? But there were no dogs in the White House. The President hated dogs.

"Can't blame him," the chief of staff muttered. Holding his reeking shoe at arm's length, he limped off in search of a new cleaning service.

That night, raucous laughter rang out from the Oval Office. Guards responded, but all they found was a tumbler with a few drops of Cutty Sark leaving marks on the Resolute desk. Imprints from cowboy boots worn by a tall man with a long stride appeared on the White House carpets but the trails led nowhere.

The president was apoplectic.

"Don't stay at Pennsylvania Avenue," he posted on social media at 3 a.m. "Noisy, dirty—not like a real Trump property."

The next morning, the president refused to enter the Oval Office. He gathered his staff in the hallway.

"Not going in there," he snapped. "Terrible office. Disgusting desk. The place is haunted! We're all going to

Mar-a-Lago. No ghosts there. Call the helicopter. Notify Air Force One."

From around the corner, the ghost of LBJ chuckled. All was going just according to plan.

His next stop was the White House pressroom where reporters from Pulitzer-winning publications, barred from a special briefing about the president's greatness, waited outside. The ghost of LBJ sidled over to a woman from *The New York Times* and slipped a big manila envelope into her briefcase. It contained papers, photos, and some of those strange little "drive" doohickies Hoover had assured him were the latest thing in communications.

LBJ watched as the reporter found the envelope, read a few pages, and then dashed into an alcove to make a call on her little handheld phone.

Johnson chuckled. Technology might change, but the FBI didn't. Hoover's operation had supplied enough damning information, some real and some maybe not so real, but plenty convincing, to blow the president higher than Trump Tower.

Damn, it was good to be back in the White House.

After letting his spectral beagles out to do their business on the White House lawn, Johnson embarked on a self-guided tour of his old stomping grounds. Sure enough, Richard Nixon—*that wimp*—had removed the high-power shower nozzles. But the secret mezzanines were still there. Johnson popped into all three of the White House kitchens to see what they were cooking these days. Seemed to be a lot of steak, which no Texan could argue with.

Late in the afternoon, the ghost slipped next door to the Executive Office Building where he left a short note for Mike Pence.

> *Restore funding for Health and Human Services programs and put someone who genuinely cares about our kids in charge of Education. Or you're next on the list, jackass.*

He appended his famous lowercase signature: *lbj.*

At the Senate Office Building, he headed for Mitch McConnell's office, where he left a more diplomatic note.

> *Mitch, I have long appreciated your crossing party lines in 1964 to vote for me to show your support for the Civil Rights Act. Yes, we're politicians. But we're also public servants who care deeply about the people of this country. All of them. Don't you think it's about time you started voting your conscience again? I'd strongly advise it.—lbj*

At dusk Johnson was back at the White House where he stepped out onto the Truman Balcony, Scotch in hand, to watch his plan for Trump come to fruition.

He'd barely had time to take a sip before two burly men in white coats appeared, escorting the ranting, raving, and writhing chief executive across the South Lawn and onto a helicopter. Staff and reporters were circling the landing pad like sharks.

The helicopter lifted off and flew into the sunset--headed northwest toward the new Walter Reed Medical Center, which, Johnson had read, had excellent mental health facilities.

"In your guts, you know he's nuts," Johnson cackled. That had been his favorite slogan from the 1964 campaign, and, wouldn't you know it, it was still true of the GOP leadership half a century later.

When he turned to go back inside, LBJ was startled and somewhat annoyed to find at his elbow the ghost of J. Edgar Hoover.

"Good God, man!" Johnson snapped, sloshing his drink. Recovering his equilibrium, he dished out his thanks.

"Great job, Hoover. Those papers and pictures and those 'drive' things of yours seem to have done the trick. He's gone, and the Democrats and Republicans can get back to work, at least when they're not busy kicking the shit out of each other. As the generals say, 'mission accomplished.' I sure as hell enjoyed the visit, but I guess it's time to for me to head on back to the ranch."

It bothered him that the former FBI chief made no reply, just raised a glass of what looked like cola in a silent toast. Johnson squinted, then grimaced.

That little peckerwood is recording me! Ah, hell. Damn politics! Even in the afterlife, some things never change.

* * *

NOTE: The pre-2017 historical incidents referenced in this story are true.

Adlai Stevenson II ran three times for president (1952, 1956, and 1960) and served as President Lyndon B. Johnson's ambassador to the United Nations. During one of presidential campaign, a college student assured Stevenson that he had "the vote of every thinking American;" Stevenson quipped in reply that he'd need a good deal more than that. Stevenson's father, U.S. vice president under Grover Cleveland, is credited with the saying "Your public servants serve you right."

Political commentator Molly Ivins wrote hundreds of columns and dozens of books, and enjoyed river rafting. She dismissed rumors of a Trump presidency in 2000, and the quote in the story from her about "the stories we don't get" is verbatim.

Walter Cronkite, famed CBS new anchor from 1962 to 1981, was one of a group of well-heeled Manhattan apartment dwellers that tried and failed to stop the construction of Trump Tower in their neighborhood in 1999.

Lyndon B. Johnson, the 36th president of the United States, was shaped by his experiences as an elementary school teacher in rural Texas. When Johnson was serving in the U.S. House of Representatives, his family lived in the same D.C. neighborhood as FBI Director J. Edgar Hoover. Johnson was credited with crafting sweeping social justice and education programs under a plan referred to as "The Great Society." A colorful Texas politician, Johnson drank Cutty Sark and drove a Lincoln convertible. He had an elaborate and expensive multi-nozzle high-powered shower installed in the private quarters of the White House—a contraption that his successor, Richard Nixon, ordered demolished and replaced with a normal shower.

FBI Director J. Edgar Hoover earned the wrath of Lady Bird Johnson when the FBI's information about the sexual activities of top Johnson aide Walter Jenkins was given to the press. Hoover is believed by historians to have collected information on U.S. presidents and used that information to control government policy while heading the FBI for nearly half a century (1924 through 1972).

Senate Majority Leader Mitch McConnell (R-Kentucky) crossed party lines in 1964 to vote for Democrat Lyndon Baines Johnson for president. McConnell, at the time an intern in the office of Republican Senator John Sherman, said he did it because Johnson's opponent, Republican Barry Goldwater, had opposed the Civil Rights Act.

Bad Memories, 2032

"They can't get rid of me. Trying, they keep trying, but, nope, won't work."

"Of course not, sir."

"Can't trust them. Not one of them. They can try all they want, make all the phone calls and write all the letters. But I'm too smart for them. We're too smart for them. Ivanka's on top if it, she keeps them in line. Fired the whole team of them a few weeks ago. Right down to the chef and that fat bitch who kept telling me what to wear. Don't see them around here any more, do you?"

"No, Mr. President. They're gone now. Can I get you anything, sir?"

"Another Diet Coke. New team in place, doing a fine job. Had Wilbur Ross over here for lunch the other day. Know him? Head of the Fed? Great guy. Really knows finance; made billions on Wall Street. Chef made steak just the way we do it at the hotel. Great cut of meat, great seasoning. Ross loved it. Said it was the best."

"Mr. President, sir, your doctor is here."

"Doctor? Another check-up? Sure, sure. Busy scheduling. Keeping busy. Keeping fit."

"How are you sleeping, Mr. President?"

"Bad night last night, Doc. Couldn't sleep at all. Phone wasn't working. Couldn't log on to that social media thing. I blame that dinner. Big state banquet. The biggest. Some terrible prime minister. Some awful guy from Teriyakistan. I let Ivanka handle him. Ivanka did great."

"Just a few questions. Do you know who the president is?"

"Do I know who's the president? Hilarious. You're some joker, Doc!"

"Do you know what year it is?"

"Do I know what year it is? Hah! Very funny! It's, ah, 2028! And we've got an election to win. Bannon's busy, you can bet on that. Man knows his job."

"Dad?"

"Hi, honey. Come on in. Doctor's just leaving. You look great, sweetie."

"Trina is going to help you get dressed, Dad."

"Who's Trina?"

"Your new assistant."

"New one? Good, good. Had to fire that other girl. Terrible. Terrible clothes. Fat. Needed to lose a lot of weight."

"Danielle's gone now, Dad. You have Trina. We all like Trina. She's going to help you get dressed."

"Gotta get dressed? Is this for another one of those state dinners? I've been in meetings all day, you know, honey. The Cabinet this morning. Can't what's-his-name handle this?"

"Dad, we have to go to this. You'll enjoy it. They're dedicating the Trump Presidential Library. It's just a few blocks away, in mid-town."

"Oh, honey, I don't want to go to a library. Bo-ring. Maybe we can drive over to Jersey, play a couple rounds."

"Here, Dad. Trina has your new blue suit. It looks great on you."

"Good tailor, only the best. Now where did you say we're going?"

"The Library, Dad. Today is the dedication for your Presidential Library. Remember how much you liked the plans we showed you?"

"The plans for the Tower? Der Scutt, great architect. Great building."

"Yes. Well, the Library is right next door to the Tower, Dad. You'll like it. Tiffany is coming to the ceremony. And

Barron. And Eric. And Donald Junior. And all the grandchildren.

"Is Melania coming?"

"No, Dad. Melania went back to...well, she lives in Paris. Don't you remember? It was right after you...well...the election."

"The election? That reminds me, we need to meet with Bannon. Haven't seen him in ages!"

"That's because he's in—ah, don't worry, I'll take care of it, Dad. I'll, ah, call Steve as soon as we get back from the Library."

"How do I look?"

"Fantastic, Dad. The car is here for us. Trina and I will help you get downstairs. Watch your step. Careful there."

"Where did you say we were going?"

"The Library."

"Sure. If you want to go the library, we'll go to the library. Say, sweetie, do you think they'll have my books? *The Art of the Deal*? *Time to Get Tough*? *Great Again*? That one I wrote with Bannon about building the wall?"

"Absolutely, Dad. I'm sure they'll have every one of them."

Unnoticed

It wasn't that people deliberately ignored me. They just didn't notice me. Or half the time they thought I was somebody else.

"Why did you guys make me so...average?"

My parents exchanged glances. Mom flushed, licked her lips, looked again at my father.

No way would I tell them what had happened. How Maia Dangerfield—tall, muscular, flame-haired Maia—had almost asked me to the dance. The key word here was "almost."

Maia had made the suggestion in the hallway between classes. Before I could answer, the bell rang and traffic swept us apart. I'd fidgeted through math class and rushed to pick up my communicator from my locker as soon as the bell rang. But when I texted Maia "sure I'll go," their answer came back "huh? who? where?"

Turned out Maia had confused me with another classmate, or confused another classmate with me, and, anyway, the other one who looked and sounded just like me was in Maia's language arts class and had accepted the dance invitation 10 minutes earlier.

Burning with embarrassment over my stupid text, I ran to the skyway and rode home. It was awful, but it was true: On every possible measure, from intelligence to looks to artistic and physical abilities, I was completely undistinguished.

* * *

"It seemed like a good idea at the time," Mom said. She looked across the dinner table at Dad for help. He was working as usual, scrolling on his tablet. "Roger?"

He finally looked over at me and sighed.

"Your mother and I were ignorant," he said. *Wow. For once, Dad was actually admitting fault.* He explained that, like most prospective parents, they'd met with a counselor and had their embryo's genetic material improved using robust DNA selected from the databanks. "We thought we were making the best choice by giving you popular, well-tested genes. We wanted you to be healthy and happy. We just wanted you to fit in."

I put my elbows on the table, and buried my face in my hands. "I can't stand it. You made me *nobody*."

"Cait, we were immigrants!" My mom leaned forward, elbows on the table, her dinner forgotten. "We'd been on a waiting list to get out of Mardour for years. We knew that if we were accepted for immigration to Savania we'd have only one child license. That meant only one child. So we wanted you to be perfect."

"But not to stand out," Dad cut in. He rationalized, "We made you pretty, and healthy, and smart."

"But not so pretty, or healthy, or smart that the Savanians would be envious." Mom's voice rose, trembling. "We didn't want...trouble."

"We didn't know." Dad took Mom's hand and squeezed— probably half to comfort her and half to get her to stop babbling. "It didn't occur to us that you would want to be, in some way, 'distinctive.'"

"So I look like five other kids in school. I even have the *same voice* as 40 of them!"

I'd tried writing, singing, and artwork. But, no surprise, my so-carefully-selected genes made sure that I had no particular talents in any of these areas.

"I don't want to be nice! I don't want to be average!" My voice rose into a scream, and my Dad, ever the meek immigrant, looked with concern at the door of the apartment, worried that neighbors might be listening. Hey, at least I wasn't speaking Mardourian. Maybe that was why they'd never taught it to me.

"We could buy you more interesting clothes," Mom said, her tone conciliatory. "You could get more tattoos. Or dye your hair."

"Mom, *everyone* has tattoos. *Everyone* dyes their hair," I grumbled. I shook my head at their cluelessness, but I'd stopped shouting.

Dad went back to his tablet and Mom gave me a brave smile. "Sweetheart," she said. "We love you. We love you just the way you are."

We ate dessert, a Savanian pechta torte—because *Sens* forbid we should eat Mardourian food—in silence. I cleared the table and Dad did the dishes.

* * *

"I want cosmetic surgery," I told them a few days later, on my way to the curtained hallway nook that served as my bedroom. I looked straight at Dad, keeping my voice modulated and my tone reasonable. "You owe it to me. I'm Mardourian. I want a Mardourian nose. And someday I'll get contacts so I can have green eyes. And a treatment to have curly hair."

"But, honey, your hair is so nice," Mom began, starting as usual with the most trivial issue.

"Lily," Dad cautioned her. He and Mom gave each other the look parents exchange when their child brings up a topic on which they have long-held and differing opinions. She furrowed her eyebrows. He arched his. She pursed her lips. He tilted his head inquisitively. Mom raised her eyebrows, and he furrowed his. Then they both shook their heads, and Dad sighed.

"Cait," he said. "We need to explain."

"Yeah. You did that already."

"No," Mom shouted, tugging Dad's arm. "Cait's not ready."

Dad stepped away from her and crossed his arms over his chest. "I think Cait is. I think we *all* are."

Wait a minute. This was supposed to be about me, about my miserable, average, life in school. But suddenly, in a moment, it changed. I'd never seen my father so serious.

"We didn't want you to look like us, to look like Mardourians," he said. "Countries were closing their ports to Mardourian refugees, accusing us of war crimes. We had to bribe the peacekeepers to even get on the resettlement list for Savania."

"It was the right decision," Mom said. "Your father and I have suffered terrible discrimination, even here in Savania. Even after changing our names to Savanian names."

"There's still political unrest, even though you might not hear much about it," Dad dropped his voice to a whisper. "Think about it, Cait. Do you have any Mardourian friends in school?"

"Sure," I started. *Dem Baxter, but, wait, they were adopted by a Savanian family. Maryanne Thompson—but her dad is Savanian.* I tried to think. There was a guy in my electronics class...

"Special cases, all of them," Dad said, even though I hadn't answered his question. "Most Mardourian families have been settled in rural...areas. And now access to those areas has been restricted. Your mother and I have friends we haven't been able to contact for several months, except by printed messages that must be sent through the government security office."

Dad's face was twisted in a weak smile. "For the time being, we're safe. And what's most important to us is that you're safe. Always."

At the hastily called school assembly three weeks later, the government agents passed me by. They picked out Dem Baxter and two classmates I didn't know. Asked for their papers. Then the agents took them by the arm and led them out up the aisle of the hushed auditorium. I'll never forget Dem looking back, searching the crowd.

Almost without thinking, I threw up my hand and called out, "I—"

An arm yanked me down into my seat. It was Maia. They held me tightly and hissed in my ear, "Shut up."

After the Security Forces van left, the teachers sent everyone back to class. As if nothing had happened. We had a quiz in math, and I couldn't write a single answer.

Maia and Maryanne were waiting for me after school and said they wanted to go for keffe, to talk about what happened. For some reason I couldn't reach Mom on the communicator, so they rode home with me on the skyway. They insisted on coming up with me to our fourth-floor apartment.

Embarrassed about my family's tiny unit, I suggested that I just drop off my backpack, check in with Mom, and then we could all go to the keffehaus on the next block.

"Sure," Maia said. I saw her looking over my head at Maryanne. We rode up in the dingy elevator and stepped out into the dim hallway. At the end of the corridor, the door to my family's unit stood open, and not in an inviting way. My friends followed me into the empty apartment.

My mother was gone. Her coat, and a suitcase, were missing.

"Look for a note," Maryanne said. She was sympathetic but her tone held no surprise. We found it under my pillow, hastily scrawled. The number of an attorney, and the message:

> "Call Mr. Lampkin—he knows what to do. We made provisions for you. We love you."

We love you, I read. And heard Mom's voice adding *just the way you are.*

Wishbone

"But don't you have grandparents, Representative Podestra?" the talk show host leaned forward in an eager posture of faux concern. "How will you explain your proposed Age Equity Act to *them*?"

My grandson, Tory Podestra, decked out in a blue suit, crisp white shirt, and camera-friendly burgundy tie, didn't even blink. He'd had media training.

"As a leader of the Third Parties Coalition, I'm committed to ensuring that everyone in the United States gets a fair share of our remaining resources," he said. "There's no question that the Olds have consumed far more than their share. The AEA actually benefits them, by ensuring that those of them who reach their 72nd year will enjoy discounted access to adequate housing, healthcare and other resources all the way through their 79th year. I think the AEA is extremely generous, when you consider how all the short-sighted Baby Boomers voted for the Trump administration in

2016 and 2024. They're the ones responsible for everything that's gone wrong. This great nation of ours can still recover—the Coalition is here to see to that—but not if young people like us have to pay endlessly to keep a bunch of old right wingers with dementia on life support. Frankly, I think the Olds should be grateful that they can at least contribute something to society by getting out of the way."

I'd watched the clip of that interview over and over, first stunned, then regretting that I'd helped send that little prick to law school. Tory had been a pushy, grabby, unpleasant child and now he'd grown up to be a political nutcase. A few weeks later, at the dentist's office, I'd actually denied that I was related to him.

"Podestra is a very common name," I told the receptionist.

As it turned out, I'd underestimated Tory. And overestimated the common sense of the voting public.

Three years later Tory's Third Parties Coalition swept the 2028 elections. And a year later, to the astonishment of the pundits and the horror of 70 million Americans 65 and older, the Age Equity Act on sailed right through Congress. It was part of a Coalition budget package that combined programs friendly to young families (affordable child healthcare and daycare, tuition-free vocational school, and billions for energy-saving mass transit) with programs near and dear to the hardcore conservatives, like expansion of the Border Patrol and more private prisons. All the funding, the Coalition promised, would come from the savings anticipated from "getting the Olds out of the way."

Of course, terrified seniors opposed the Act. But what could we do? The UN passed a resolution condemning the Act, but since the U.S. no longer belonged to the UN, that barely made the news. The AARP and humanitarian groups filed suit but the Supreme Court refused to hear any of the cases. (Its members, along with other government officials, were conveniently exempt from the provisions of the AEA.) The Act went into effect in 2030.

Outpatient surgery centers leaped to add End of Life centers to their services. There were protests, of course, but after a year or so those just kind of dwindled away. You know how it is. People got busy protesting other controversial government actions, like the repeal of food safety regulations.

My family was bitterly divided over Tory's role in the passage of the AEA. My son Jason supported his son, at least publicly. My grand-daughter Zipporah, who'd always been at odds with her older half-brother, used the millions she'd earned as a high-tech executive to support the unsuccessful challenges to the AEA.

I was furious at Tory, but frightened as well. Old people living on their own were being picked up in sweeps or "processed" if they turned up at an emergency room and their health coverage had expired. Families were scrambling to calculate if they could afford to house, feed and care for their elders once Social Security and Medicare had been cut off. Of course, the ultra-wealthy were sending their grandparents out of the U.S. to high-end "elder havens" springing up in the Caribbean. But Tory and his Coalition colleagues insisted, as a point of pride, that their own grandparents would report to End of Life Centers "just like everyone else."

That meant I'd be reporting to an End of Life center next Wednesday, a week before my 80th birthday. (The original version of the Age Equity Act had mandated exterminating old folks *on* their 80th birthdays. But it turned out that requirement not only looked tacky, but involved complicated scheduling and weekend overtime. They'd fixed it so you could report for euthanization any time in your 79th year. Or even earlier! How convenient. Save society even more money.)

Needless to say, Tory didn't make an appearance at what would be my final Thanksgiving.

I'd always loved Thanksgiving, so it broke my heart that my last one was so crummy. Jason and Alicia's dining room was right out of a design blog—but the food? The turkey was overcooked, the cranberry sauce canned, the stuffing soggy, the gravy thin and slightly burnt, and the pumpkin pie store-bought. And the conversation wasn't much better.

"Anybody want to make a wish?" My son Jason, at the head of the table, wrenched the wishbone out of the turkey carcass and waved it in the air. All heads turned toward me. There was an awkward silence and everyone got busy with their food again.

After dinner I was very careful not to limp as I carried a pile of dishes out to the kitchen. Jason might rationalize that they were "putting me out of my misery," or some such thing. My daughter-in-law Alicia took the dishes from me and set them next to her fancy new farmhouse sink. "Vivian, Jason and I really do want to be with you Wednesday when you go to the center," she said.

"That's very kind of you, but I've made other arrangements."

"But—"

"Mom, I'm taking her." Zipporah closed the refrigerator door and leaned back against the quartzite countertop, casual in her black hoodie and faded jeans. "Grandma and I talked about it, and it's all set."

While my granddaughter speaks in a soft, low voice, the woman means business. My late husband Eric had been so proud of Zipporah, with her engineering degree and the two companies she'd founded. He would have applauded her decision to live "off the grid" in a community of environmental activists in the mountains outside Bellingham. And he would have been intrigued by her plan to rescue me from the AEA.

I had to hope that it would work.

* * *

"They have no idea what we're up to, do they?" I said as

we jounced along in Zipporah's hybrid truck, headed for my apartment.

"No idea at all," Zipporah said, her tone grim. "That's my mom and dad. Follow the rules."

"Your dad was that way even as a kid," I told her. "Anything to keep the peace."

"It drove them crazy that Tory and I fought all the time," she said. "But did they ever do anything to stop him bullying me? Oh, no, it was always 'an accident' and we should 'just get along.' You and Grampa were the only grownups who ever stood up for me."

No wonder Zipporah had always wanted to stay with us on the weekends. I hadn't realized it had been that bad with her half-brother. "Well, now you're more than paying me back."

"It's the least I can do, Grandma." Zipporah cranked the steering wheel and the truck splashed through a puddle into the parking lot of my retirement community.

"Are you coming up to take the boxes?" I asked her. A dozen boxes sat in my living room, packed with clothes and books.

"Yes, but we have to be careful what we say once we're inside the building." Zipporah shut off the engine. "It's possible that your apartment has been bugged. Having you comply with the AEA, having you die, is essential for Tory's career. Tory can't have his political opponents saying that his grandmother got special treatment."

* * *

Jason and Alicia came over to my apartment Tuesday night to say goodbye.

"I'm so sorry about this, Mom," Jason said. "I really, really am.

"I'm know," I said. "Hey, maybe Tory's smart. Maybe it's better this way than me ending up in a nursing home."

Jason, completely missing my sarcasm, brightened. "Tory's running for—" Alicia yanked at his arm, but he didn't notice "—president, you know."

What? My mouth opened and closed.

"Jason!" Alicia glared at him.

"Yeah, not supposed to say anything, but she..."

Yeah, but I'll be dead tomorrow.

Jason raised his shoulders sheepishly. We had another round of awkward hugs, Alicia dried a tear or two, and they were off for, well, forever—as far as they were concerned. I changed into pajamas and poured some apricot brandy into an old juice glass that hadn't been worth packing.

Maybe I should just end it, after all. I'd lived 80 years. Taught English at three colleges. Never got tenure, but had some amazing students. Married someone I loved, raised a son, and then outlived my husband. I'd lucked out, thus far, in terms of my own health. Only a few skin cancers and the arthritis.

Why not quit now, while I'm ahead? All I'd have to do was let them give me those two injections at the Center tomorrow and it would be over. I could thank Zipporah for her generous offer but tell her I'd changed my mind.

* * *

They gave me the first injection in the side of my neck. I tried to relax, staring into the eyes of the young doctor.

"You'll feel sleepy soon, Vivian." He patted my hand.

But I didn't feel sleepy. I felt perfectly fine. I counted my last conscious breaths. *Not sleepy.* Something must be wrong. I shifted in the chair. I could move, but not very far. They'd strapped me in, a belt across my lap and another across my chest.

"You should be feeling sleepy now," the doctor said. He turned away. A nurse handed him the second syringe, and he held it up to the bright ceiling light for a moment.

"But I don't," I protested. "I don't feel sleepy. And I don't want to do this."

I struggled, held down by the straps. The young doctor, who looked much like Tory, loomed over me. "You've used too many resources already, Vivian."

"No!" I shouted. "I don't want to die. Zipporah! Help!"

* * *

I woke from the nightmare absolutely sure I wanted to go through with Zipporah's plan, a plan that should enable me to stay alive until the natural, not legislated, end of my life.

Zipporah arrived at my place at 8 a.m. carrying a bag of cinnamon sugar donuts and a thermos of coffee. We ate at the kitchen table, keeping our faces blank and not saying much. If anyone was watching or listening, it looked convincingly like a somber "last breakfast."

"Did you know—" I began. Zipporah put her finger to her lips.

I wrote on a slip of paper: *Tory is running for president.*

Yes, she wrote back. *Not to worry.*

She knew! I concentrated on swallowing a bite of donut. Then I rinsed the cups and said a quiet goodbye to the kitchen. We took my keys down to the main office, where people didn't have much to say either. They knew where I was going.

In the truck, Zipporah turned to me. "I need to level with you, Grandma. I know the plan was just to fake the euthanasia and take you up to the farm and hide you," she said. "But we have a tremendous opportunity to stop Tory's presidential campaign—and the Third Party Coalition. Well, *you* have the opportunity."

I listened as Zipporah explained the plan.

"Let's give it a try," I said.

* * *

A half-dozen protesters stood clustered at the entrance of the End of Life Center. Their signs read, "Don't tell US when to die!" and "Someday your grandkids will do this to YOU!" As Zipporah and I walked past, they bowed their heads in silence.

"God bless," one woman called out.

I did my best to look grim and brave. At the front desk I showed my driver's license and signed forms that said that I understood that the medication I'd be given would result in death.

Zipporah squeezed my hand, and they led me away to the windowless room. With a Formica-topped counter and a beige padded surgical chair, it looked uncomfortably like the room in my nightmare. Two large syringes lay on a white tray on the counter. One to put me to sleep, the other to stop my heart. I frowned. This was a bit too realistic.

The nurse came in, a thin woman, nondescript in aqua scrubs. She motioned me to the chair. I thought it was strange that she didn't meet my gaze. She was supposed to be a friend of Zipporah's, but...

My heart pounded.

To my relief, the nurse held a finger to her lips and pointed to a dressing area with a curtain. I peeked in and saw, not a gown, but a set of blue cotton scrubs hanging from a hook. Beside them was an ID badge on a lanyard. A brown wig lay on a bench. And there was an exit door.

I donned the disguise and read the typed note tucked under the wig.

Leave your clothes. Take the clipboard and follow the hall to the tunnel. Go into Room 122, open the outside door, and wait for a blue Subaru SUV.

The tunnel was long and dim. A medical technician headed the other way took no notice of me. I found Room 122—but where was the blue SUV?

Finally, the car appeared and I hurried out. The driver, a round-faced young woman in a red ski jacket, grinned. "Fancy spaghetti for lunch?" she asked.

That was the pass phrase I'd been told to wait for. "Sounds great," I said, and collapsed into the passenger seat. I was headed into my second life—as a fugitive.

But two police cars, along with a van from a local TV station and several photographers, were waiting for us in the front parking lot. Zipporah was there, too—tall and angry, waving her arms at the police officers. When our car stopped, Zipporah yanked open the passenger door and pulled me out.

"Grandma!" she wailed. "They've caught us!" Her cheeks were streaked with tears. I was astonished. I didn't think

I'd seen Zipporah cry since she was six and Tory had stomped on her collection of toy ponies.

With a great show of choking back tears, my granddaughter faced the cameras. "We love our grandmother, and Tory couldn't bear the thought of Vivian dying because of his Age Equity Act. He was able to set up a plan to smuggle her out of country. You really can't blame my brother for saving his own, dear, grandmother, can you?"

I attempted to look as grandmotherly as possible while the cameras circled around us and the reporters shouted questions.

* * *

The headlines the next morning were brutal:

Podestra Caught Smuggling Grandma to Safety!

Accusations of Family Favoritism Sink Podestra Campaign

Tory protested his innocence. But no one believed him. Zipporah and her hacker friends had set up a perfect frame, right down to sending a huge payment from one of Tory's bank accounts to an "elder haven" in Costa Rica. Those boxes of possessions I'd given Zipporah the previous week? Why, they'd mysteriously been delivered to Tory's house in Chevy Chase. The reporters spotted them on the front porch.

Just as Zipporah and her friends had hoped, the scandal they'd cooked up put an end to Tory's presidential campaign. He had to resign his congressional seat in the face of outrage from Coalition colleagues whose own families had sacrificed grandparents and parents to his Age Equity Act. But, most importantly, the uproar led Congress to rescind the Act itself.

* * *

"Congratulations all around, and especially to our new neighbor, Vivian!" Zipporah's friends toasted me at a belated Thanksgiving dinner. There were ten of us eating a heritage turkey raised right here on the farm. The cranberry sauce was homemade, there was plenty of thick gravy, and I'd cooked fettucine with mushrooms and a green bean casserole for the vegetarians. Zipporah took the turkey wishbone out to the kitchen to dry in the oven and came back carrying a warm apple pie.

We talked late into the night about candidates, about issues, about the importance of registering voters and getting out the vote. A young woman pointed out the advantages of moving even further off the grid.

"Forget the system. We can grow our own food, run our own schools," she argued. "We can live better than most Americans."

I had to say something. "Going off the grid may be a solution for you, but what about—well, what about everyone else? People who can't afford land? People who are disabled? People who are old? Remember, you'll all be old someday—at least, I hope you will."

Zipporah tapped me on the shoulder. She held out the oven-dried wishbone to me. I grasped my end between thumb and forefinger and closed my eyes. I was wishing for good health and long life with my new family. Zipporah was probably wishing for a whole new political system.

Would she get her wish, or would I get mine? It didn't matter. Either way, things would be better.

The wishbone snapped...

Politics As Usual

"We can't let evil change our life and change our schedule."

—U.S. President Donald Trump, October 27, 2018, in the wake of the Pittsburgh synagogue killings.

There was no way to trace the communications. The code words had been set up months ago and distributed online through closed groups.

Now, someone was broadcasting the code words through public channels—and the terrorists went into action.

It began with a massacre at an urban synagogue in late October—the first in a 10-day series of massacres leading up to national elections.

Each shooting and bombing took place in a blue city, where voters traditionally supported Democratic or progressive candidates. No shootings took place in the red suburbs.

Each shooting was perpetrated by a man quickly described as "a lone shooter with a history of mental illness."

Each of the shooters drove vans covered in the same political stickers and each wore the same uniform: A motley assembly of second-hand military and security gear with a bulletproof vest.

Every shooter was captured alive. Despite being heavily armed, they offered little or only token resistance to the police. One reporter's smartphone captured a shooter addressing the officer who led him from the scene as "Brother." The officer grimaced.

Public defenders represented the shooters at their bail hearings. But David Means, a freelance journalist for several liberal news blogs, discovered that the legal papers subsequently filed with the courts were all signed by criminal defense attorneys from the same major law firm.

"Where are these 'lone shooters' getting the money to hire these lawyers?" Means asked on one of his obscure blogs. "Or, why is this particular firm offering legal defense services for free?" Larger papers failed to pick up this story, scrambling as they were to prepare in case the next shooting took place in one of their own cities.

Election Day began with a mass killing in a New England college. Fifty students, professors, and university employees were mowed down as they waited in line to vote outside the college's divinity school. Soon the internet was flooded with pictures of young students on their knees beside fallen friends on the leaf-strewn sidewalk, in stark silhouette against a row of classic white New England buildings.

"Terror at the Polls," the headlines blared.

Within minutes, tens of thousands of people nationwide went online to demand that the elections be halted.

"We fear for our lives if we try to vote!" one teacher wrote.

"I've risked my life for my country in the field," a veteran posted. "Now I have to do it while voting."

Democratic leaders, citing the string of attacks on blue cities, charged voter suppression.

"Unfortunately, closing the polls is a state and local decision, outside our purview," a spokesperson for the Federal Elections Commission said. Three of the commissioners decried the situation as "voter intimidation." But the other three dismissed the campus killings as "an isolated incident," pointing out that the 10 preceding mass killings had not taken place at a polling place and had nothing to do with the elections.

Rumors—true? unfounded?—raced through the internet. There were rumors that polling places in Tulsa, Austin, Dallas, Nashville, Boston, Miami and other major cities would be targeted in the next few hours. Tens of thousands of people in those cities posted that they were cancelling plans to go to the polls for fear of being shot.

Meanwhile, tens of thousands of people in red precincts posted pictures of themselves exiting their polling places, holding up printed signs that read, "I'M not AFRAID to VOTE." (Where had they gotten those signs? Means asked two voters exiting the polls in his own suburban town. "I don't know—I guess they just had them at the polls, somewhere," one man answered.)

Election officials throughout the country were wringing their hands. No one was prepared take the responsibility for closing polling places on Election Day. Administration officials issued statements insisting that "Americans will not be intimidated by an isolated incident in a tiny college town." In many states, officials urged people to "Stay alert," and promised police presence at polling stations.

There was a collective sigh of relief when the polls closed at 8 p.m. on the West Coast.

"Not a single ADDITIONAL mass shooting has occurred," Means posted. "And sadly, in this country, that constitutes 'good' news."

In urban areas, voter turnout was down 30 to 50 percent from the previous presidential election's levels. In suburban and rural areas, it was down 3 percent. Nearly every progressive challenger to a conservative incumbent was solidly defeated. (The only exceptions were in Oregon, where mail-in voting had taken place weeks earlier.) The president won re-election and claimed the Electoral College by a landslide.

"We are not afraid! We are not afraid! We did not let the actions of one single lone person, one guy who's acting completely alone, with a clear history of not being mentally in good shape, get in the way of us voting for, voting for and electing, the very best candidates, real winners, in our great country," the president said in a speech the following morning.

"It's business as usual," the White House spokesperson told reporters. "We will not be intimidated."

The White House issued no official statement that night when a bomb went off in the basement of an inner-city church in Baltimore that had been used as a polling place the previous day. The explosion destroyed the building, injuring a janitor who'd been cleaning the pastor's office.

"Some people just can't keep on schedule," the president posted on social media that night. But that post quickly vanished.

The Bodies We Carry

My husband stopped breathing just after midnight. Kaylee and I sat by the bed for several minutes choking on our sighs and sobs. The wind that had rattled the windows of the house during our vigil had died as well. We were left floating in a pool of silence.

"Go ahead, Mom." Kaylee squeezed my hand. "You promised. You promised Dad."

I shook my head in despair and disbelief. But Kaylee was right. I'd promised to take my husband's cancer-ravaged body to the Lakeshore Dead Camp.

"Hey, Kath, check this out," Dean had said when he saw the first news story about the camps.

I'd listened as I cleared our breakfast dishes, shaking my head in incredulity as he explained. Some group calling themselves Campers for Care had obtained the home addresses of the CEOs and board members of major insurance companies, drug companies, and hospitals.

Dean grinned. "They're taking dead bodies to their offices. To the lobbies of their beachfront condos. They put three dead bodies on the dock of this guy's vacation place. This is great."

I rolled my eyes. "Come on, Dean. I seriously doubt the cities are letting them do this."

Dean steadied his laptop on bony knees. "No, it says here that San Francisco and Denver are giving the Campers permission to keep the bodies on site, in body bags, for up to 36 hours. And there's been what they call a 'dead camp' going on for nearly two weeks in front of some pharma CEO's mansion in Chicago."

"You don't really—" But I stopped. I hadn't seen that glint in my husband's eyes for months.

"Kath, seriously, this is perfect for me," he said. "I'll be dead in a month or two, and they say they're going to start up some camps in Seattle. Let's just keep the possibility in mind. Please?"

So I started reading up on the dead camps, mostly to figure out how to talk Dean out of his crazy idea. When I came across the list of billionaire healthcare investors being targeted by the Seattle Campers, my heart seized. *Jeffrey Kase.* Jeff lived here, in Seattle? I hadn't known. Well, he and I certainly ran in different circles these days. Anyway, the Campers were setting up in front of his lakefront mansion in an exclusive neighborhood.

I asked Dean if he was sure he wanted me to take his body to Jeff Kase's lawn.

"Absolutely! Bet Jeff will be surprised to see *you* again." He'd had another bad night and his voice was only a whisper.

"Oh, I doubt he'd even recognize me." I hardly recognized myself these days—my hair straggly, my body slack. I'd been juggling three contract gigs to pay the mortgage while the bills for Dean's palliative care piled up on the dining room table.

"Oh yes he will! Kath, sweetie—how could anyone forget you?" Dean smiled.

I smiled back, which was hard to do without crying. Dean was sleeping most of the time now. I bathed him, cleaned him, fed him liquids from a dropper, and tried to reassure Kaylee. We administered the painkilling opioids brought by the hospice nurse who came for a few minutes each day. We couldn't afford inpatient care, but Dean wanted to die at home, anyway.

A doctor I'd never met before came and made out a death certificate. I lied and told the doctor that I'd also called a funeral home; they'd be by in an hour. No, we didn't need the hospice counselor. No, really, thanks.

Ten minutes later, an unmarked utility van backed into our driveway. Two women from the Campers helped me maneuvered Dean's body into a heavy grey body bag. The three of us carried it out to the van. It was 3 a.m.

When we drove past an abandoned shopping mall, I thought about that senator who'd referred to the bodies at the dead camps as "zombies." Dean would have loved to come back as a zombie! I stifled hysterical laughter. He'd have shambled off immediately to eat the brains of the asshole boss who had fired him—oh, excuse me, *laid him off*—when he got cancer.

The van turned onto a gently curving, tree-lined street, and there it was: The Lakeshore Dead Camp. It filled the broad parking strip, body bags and blankets spilling over onto the landscaped front lawns. Our van parked under a streetlight. A man and a woman stood up from a sidewalk folding table and came over to greet us. The tall Black woman wearing a faded army jacket and a red armband introduced herself as Mikela. She handed me a clipboard with a registration form.

I signed that I'd agree to have Jeff's body picked up and removed by the funeral director who worked with the camp within 36 hours.

"We're the site supervisors for the overnight shift." Mikela spoke softly. Her hands were gentle as she took my wrist and fastened a neon-green plastic band. It was marked with the date and time, thirty-six hours from now, when Dean would be picked up by the funeral home. She leaned into the van and put a matching tag on the grey body bag. Then she and the other supervisor, a heavyset man with elaborate tattoos, helped me carry Dean to the wide parking strip in front of a three-story Italianate mansion.

Jeff Kase's house.

I sniffed, registered an unpleasant decay, and put my hand over my nose.

Mikela saw me and shook her head. "No, it's not the bodies. It's from the lake. It's low. But *some* people let their imaginations run away with them…" She tilted her head to indicate a police car at the far end of the block. Although the night was cool, even chilly, the cops had the engine running, windows up, and the air conditioner on.

I looked down at the dark, rumpled bag at our feet and wondered what on earth I was doing here. I shook my head, as if coming out of a dream. Mikela nodded as if she knew what I was thinking.

"Can I get you anything?" she asked.

"Not now. But thank you."

Across the street, one of the tall double doors of a modern house creaked opened and we looked over.

"Oh, great. It's *him* again," Mikela said.

A silver-haired man in a dark blue track suit hurried down the steps of the house with two slim Dobermans scrabbling on tight leashes. He headed right for us, but stopped in the middle of the street.

"You people still here?" he said. "I've called the mayor's office. I'm meeting with the governor. You're going to get this disgusting health hazard off our lawns or I'm calling in private security." The two dogs whined, straining at their leashes, tongues lolling.

Mikela said nothing.

Yanking the dogs back, the man walked down the street to the patrol car. The cops rolled down the window and listened, nodding, as the man talked for several minutes, making expansive gestures with his free arm.

"Sorry about that," Mikela said. "That asshole turned a hose on us two nights ago The cops stopped him, and we're keeping an eye on him now."

I opened my duffle, took out my coat, and settled down beside my husband's body. Before I knew it, it was light. Other Campers stopped by to introduce themselves and ask about Dean. Two women had brought the bodies of suicides—a brother who'd been unable to afford insulin and an aunt who'd been denied coverage for mental health treatment. In the early afternoon, a daughter arrived with the body of her 74-year-old father who'd died of an infection that swept through his understaffed nursing home.

Only the young woman a few feet away from me kept silent. She sat cross legged with head bowed, her long, mousy brown hair hiding her face. She ignored the volunteers who came by every few hours distributing alcohol wipes, water, and sandwiches. I thought it was strange that there was no body bag at her side. But then I saw that she cradled a small blue bundle. She snuggled it, murmured to it, and released her grip only to take a sip from a large thermos. When she went to use the portable toilet the Campers had placed in the street beside their van, she tucked the small bundle into a quilted pink sling and carried it with her.

When night fell, I lay down beside Dean's body. Following the Campers' instructions, I'd packed a heavy, hooded winter coat. As the night grew cold, I shrugged into it, pulled up the hood, and used it as sleeping bag. "Goodnight, sweetie," I murmured to Dean, a resting shape beside me. That's what I'd always said, why not say it now? "I hope this is what you wanted."

He didn't answer.

I woke at 3 a.m. to see a man standing over me, silhouetted against the streetlight. At first I thought he was with the Campers, but then I noticed his clothes. He wore a long plaid bathrobe, jogging pants, and leather slippers.

"Katherine?" he said.

I gaped. It had never occurred to me that Jeff Kase would come out to the Dead Camp. I guess I'd assumed he and his family would have gone away to one of their other houses. I'd fantasized about confronting him in a courtroom, a government hearing room, even a political talk show. But not on his lawn in the middle of the night.

"Katherine?"

"Yes." I struggled to sit up, the down coat falling from my shoulders. I hadn't seen Jeff since college graduation. We'd broken up the night before, after a long, tearful conversation in a tree-lined courtyard. He'd gone off to business school. I'd gone to my first job.

"I saw you out here this afternoon." He knelt on his lawn beside me and my dead husband. "I am so very, very sorry." He held out a sleek silver thermos. "I...I thought you might need some cocoa."

Did you make the cocoa, or do you have servants for that?

He twisted off the thermos lid. This cocoa even smelled expensive. Jeff pulled a ceramic mug from the pocket of his robe, filled it with cocoa, and held it out.

"Thanks," I said automatically.

He pulled out a second mug and poured cocoa for himself.

Negotiating tactic. Like having a drink with the upset stockholder. My fingers tightened on my mug.

Jeff said nothing while I sipped his cocoa. It was OK. It was good. Actually, it was the best cocoa I'd ever had. To my horror, I felt tears rolling down my cheeks. My back began to shake.

"I'm sorry, Katherine," he said.

I swallowed, leaned away from him, and choked out what I'd planned to say. "We couldn't afford the insurance and the drugs. *Your* insurance, *your* drugs."

Jeff waited a few beats to respond.

Media training.

"If I'd known, I'd have helped you," he said.

"Oh, I'd have let you." I thought about that one moment of hope, when one of Dean's experimental chemotherapies had worked. I would have let Jeff pay for that. "But now it's too late."

He left a long pause.

I gulped cocoa.

Then he tilted his head toward Dean's body. "Your life was good?"

I knew right away what he meant. He wanted to know if I'd loved Dean as much as I'd once loved him. I had. I nodded, smiling beneath my tears as I said, "Yeah. It was good. We traveled, we worked for a couple tech companies in California, and then we moved up to Seattle to be near my family after our daughter, Kaylee, was born. Dean worked for one of the big Microsoft subcontractors. I taught data architecture at the university. Then..."

I shook my head. I bit my lip. I looked up at the stars as though I could fly up to them and leave this world. Then

I took a deep breath and came to grips with the fact that I was still here. In this extraordinary place: surrounded by dead bodies and talking to one of the people responsible for their needlessly painful and expensive deaths. A man I'd once been in love with. Back in the days when we all were young and healthy.

"The cancer destroyed everything," I whispered. "He lost his job. I lost my job because I ran out of leave to care for him. I tried to freelance. We went through our retirement savings. Stopped paying bills. Now he's gone. He's *gone*."

This time, I looked right at Jeff as I spoke. He sat across from me, and the streetlight showed only the side of his face, leaving his eyes in shadow. He looked so much younger than I did: A tan, probably cosmetic surgery, an expensive haircut. A touch of silver glinted in his thick, wavy hair. I'd read he was on his third wife. He didn't meet my gaze, and my heart sank. When he said nothing, I went on, "Sick people commit suicide to save their families from going bankrupt."

I saw him stiffen, repelled by my ugly words, but I couldn't stop. "Two people here did that. But I made Dean promise me to stay with us for as long as possible. And that cost us everything we had. How about you, Jeff? Ever lost anything? Or do you just buy replacements?"

Jeff looked in the distance and shook his head. After a long silence he said, "You know, all I wanted, *all I wanted*, was a career in finance and somehow I've ended up as the sort of guy who has dead bodies on their lawn?

Apparently so. Anyway, I have a son. He's working for the Campers. He won't speak to me."

I saw an opening and went for it. "Your son—does that mean you're going to do something about it?"

Jeff spoke as if talking to himself. "I've been focused on numbers for years, better and better numbers. The healthcare companies I invest in—they have to meet the same standards as manufacturing, or oil drilling, or technology. People keep buying health insurance, so I figure the product is a good one. It's still somewhat hard for me to believe that people who purchase good insurance aren't getting the care they need. I mean—"

"Get real." I settled the mug of cocoa in the grass. "There is no 'good' insurance any more. We need insurance that actually covers people instead of denying their claims. Insurance that doesn't have sky-high deductibles. Insurance that doesn't tell you everything you need is out of network. Insurance that's affordable for—"

"Yeah. I know, I know." The voice of the impatient executive cut me off.

No surprise there.

"Katherine, it's complicated. It's going to take time. You're going for headlines by targeting a few CEOS like me, but what about the investment guys, and the big shareholders, like Bob Richardson across the street?" Jeff wave his hand in the direction of the house with the two Dobermans. "You think *they* care what you're doing?

You've got great intentions, but you're wasting your time."

"Wasting time?" Now my voice was a snarl. "You'll find that dead people, and those of us who've lost them, have all the time in the world. And we'll stay out here on your goddamn lawn until you people fucking do something."

Jeff sniffed. "Well, you may be out here a while."

In the silence that followed, I heard the young woman with the baby, sitting just behind him, stir. There was a loud *crack!* Then Jeff gasped and fell forward onto the grass.

I looked up to see the woman, one arm clasping her dead baby, the other extended, pointing a gun. Her thin face was a terrible, grinning mask.

Shouts filled the night. The site supervisors came running, flashlights bobbing. People scrambled to their feet. A police radio crackled.

Jeff moaned. When I put my hand to his shoulder, my fingers came away wet, smelling metallic. *Blood.*

Mikela held the girl by the shoulders, careful not to touch the tiny, shrouded body she cradled. The other supervisor was kneeling by Jeff. A cop barked into her radio. "One of them shot a homeowner."

"Jeffrey Kase," I called out. "His name is Jeffrey Kase."

"Kase!" A man's voice from across the lawn. "The insurance company guy. I hope he dies!"

"No!" I said. *He wants to help.*

But did he? Would he, after this? No one would believe me about Jeff's intentions if he died. Sirens wailed and a cop pounded on the front door of Jeff's house. Lights came on.

A woman in a long pale robe stood silhouetted in the doorway, her arms crossed.. "You must be mistaken." Her voice was calm. "My husband's in his study." She turned and called, "Jeffrey! Jeffrey!"

She can't believe he came out to our camp.

Two EMTs sprinted through the maze of bodies and Campers.

"Everybody back," the cop shouted. "Back!"

But I stayed by Dean's body, protecting him as the wheels of the stretcher rattled past.

The ambulance left. Cops with notepads and flashlights lumbered among us. I gave my name and said only that the homeowner had offered me a cup of cocoa. I raised the mug as proof. The cop took down my name and address, then moved to the next camper.

Across the street the older man with the Dobermans— Bob Richardson, Jeff had said his name was—was out on the sidewalk in his bathrobe. He had no dogs with him now. He stood beneath a streetlight and frowned as the Campers' van pulled up with another dead body. He was alone, I noticed. Always alone. And now I wondered if he, too, had lost someone.

Ask him. This time I heard Dean's voice clearly. Still there, with his practical solutions.

"Keep an eye on me, sweetheart," I whispered to Dean.

Always.

And I crossed the street to start a conversation.

A Sign of the Times

Kate Morales' office wasn't much to look at. The dark furniture and leather chairs were new, but you could see peeling paint and hear the old radiators wheezing to keep the place warm on a rainy afternoon. They'd said she was good with my kind of case. And that I could, possibly, afford her.

My brother Pete refused to go with me. He'd paid my bail, but after that he asked me to contact him only through the number of a burner phone he'd purchased. "Sorry, man. It's just too dangerous these days."

So I'd taken the bus downtown by myself. Kate's office was in the Smith Tower. It's gone now, but it used to be a Seattle landmark. Just two blocks from the old courthouse.

"Mr. Henry?" Kate stood up to greet me, but when I nodded, she sat back down in her chair and began rummaging through papers on her desk. Short dark hair.

Her nose not quite right for pretty—a little large, a bit crooked. Big brown eyes that, I'd learn, could go from warm to chill in a heartbeat.

Derek, the law student who worked for her then, offered me a coffee. I shook him off, having no taste for stuff from an office coffee machine (how I wish I could have a cup of that now!). I sat down in one of the two leather chairs that faced Kate's desk. I realized, as I tried to get comfortable, that most people had someone who came with them. But Pete wouldn't get involved and Alison— well, I hadn't heard from her since my arrest and the news people came to her house wanting to know things about me.

I sat with my hands on my knees and looked down. I noticed how my suit seemed kind of baggy. I hadn't worn a suit since Pete's wedding, 14 years earlier. I guess I'd lost weight. Or maybe the styles had changed. Most I wore jeans, but that hadn't seemed right for an attorney's office.

There was a soft sigh as Kate opened a file folder on her desk. I looked up to see her biting her lip.

"That bad?" I said, giving her a nervous grin.

"Well..." Kate closed the file, shaking her head. "Mr. Henry. There's no way you're going to get off. But, since it's a first offense, I'm looking for ways we can get the prosecutor to reduce the charges."

She must have seen the hope on my face. She shook her head, sadly. "Unfortunately, it seems as though the new prosecutor wants to make a test case out of this. He's thrown a lot at you, most of it charged under the state's new Corporate Hate Crimes laws."

"So you're going to tell me to plead? I can. I mean, I did—"

"Let's hold on a minute." Kate leaned back in her chair. I studied her blue suit, her plain pink blouse, her tiny gold earrings. Her eyes read the wall above my head. "This is your first arrest, right?"

I nodded.

"We'd did a check and it looks like you have a clean record. College degree. Steady work as an engineer at a series of boatyard and fishing industry jobs around Seattle and Bellingham. You own a house in Bellfair. Divorced 10 years back. No children, no child support. Girlfriend?"

"Ye—" Then I remembered about Alison. "Not anymore."

"Sorry about that. Arrests?"

I shook my head.

"No other names? Other than Joseph Henry?"

"No other names. But I've done some things, before, that would probably get me arrested these days."

Kate ignored my chuckle. She bit her lip again and picked up another file folder. "My investigator looked at your social media. Lots of pictures of you at marches and rallies protesting the closing of Lake Union to create a private business park for three of Seattle's largest companies. I'm sure the prosecutor has found a lot more." She gave me a sharp look. "Were you involved in the May 2023 riots?"

Finally I could give her some good news. "Early halibut run that year, so I was up in Alaska, getting a friend's boat ready."

Kate was nodding now, staring again at the files on her desk. "So it's really just this incident." We sat in silence as she picked up the arrest report again. "Unfortunately, Joe, the violation is clear. Pictures went viral. They showed you standing in front of Feracidata company headquarters, holding that sign."

It read:

> *Destroy Feracidata! Take back our jobs, our environment, and our city!*

"Did someone maybe, you know, just suddenly give you that sign to carry? Shove it into your hands?" Kate asked, her voice rising at the possibility. "That would be a major, exonerating issue."

I hated to discourage her. "I made the sign myself. In my garage."

Kate exchanged a quick look with Derek. His long, bony face twisted in a grimace. "And I suppose you still have the paints in there," she said, her voice trailing off.

"Yes."

Derek grunted, got up and left the room. Kate shuffled papers again. I started to suspect she was just buying time.

"How bad is it?" I asked.

"Well, there isn't a lot of case law. The state statutes only went into effect six months ago. The prosecutor is arguing that the sign—your sign—was featured in local news coverage and that, as a result, it incited the riots that culminated in the firebombing of the Ferocidata conference center two night later."

"No one got hurt."

"True. But under the new Washington State statue, corporations are regarded by the law as individuals, and advocating any action to harm them is a hate crime. You're going to be a test case."

"Yeah. Got it. I mean, I'll plead guilty. I'm ready to take my punishment."

"No." Kate snapped, her voice bringing Derek back into the room. "Joe, if you're convicted of advocating violence against the corporation, violence that clearly took place—"

"Prison?"

Kate looked right at me, for the first time, as if she thought I might be joking. One eyebrow went up. "Prison?" She gave a short, ugly laugh. "Under the new statute, the judge has no sentencing discretion. And law says the penalty for publicly proposing violence against a corporation is death."

I didn't think I'd heard her right. She asked more questions. I mumbled some answers. She said she'd take my case and that I should refer any journalists' inquiries to her. I signed lots of papers. One of them authorized her to apply to outside agencies for funding for the case—her fees, investigators' fees, research fees.

To my amazement, in the following months, tens of thousands of dollars flowed in. Money kept coming in, all though the trial and, I guess, after my conviction when Kate brought in all those specialist lawyers to do the appeals. By then I was in the Washington State Penitentiary in Walla Walla, where the state houses Death Row prisoners.

Three years later, when Washington outsourced its long-term incarceration to Texas, they moved me. Strange the way it was almost frightening to be outside the walls. It was a bleak November night. They put ten of us onto a beat-up looking plane that must have been chartered. Kept us handcuffed, seated far apart from each other. It was still dark when we landed in Houston, got in a bus, and they drove us out here to West Livingston.

Turns out Texas pretty much specializes in Death Row prisoners these days. When I got here in 2035 there were more than 300 men, and now, we're up to nearly 400. Most of them convicted of murder, but more than 30 guys like me, charged under state Corporate Hate

Crimes laws. By now, more than 30 states have them and in 18 states, a conviction mandates the death penalty.

The attorney who took over for Kate when she retired tells me that more women than men get convicted for corporate hate crimes. I wonder why that is.

What do I do these days? I read books—mostly science fiction. I sketch plans for boats I'd like to build. And I wonder—a lot—about all the things I never tried or did while I was on the outside and could have done any of them, at any time. Always meant to summit Mount Rainier. Spend a weekend on the Oregon Coast.

During the appeals, I stayed busy answering letters from researchers and journalists. At first, there were all sorts of people writing books and articles about the Corporate Hate Crimes cases. I guess they wanted to talk to the first guy who got convicted.

That's fallen off quite a bit, though. These days, what letters I do get come from researchers outside the United States. Denmark. Norway. Even Italy. *Carissime signore*, they call me! I like that. *Carissime signore…*

No, folks in the United States don't talk much about the Corporate Hate Crimes laws any more. Seems like it's dangerous even to write about them. So I guess you're the only one who'll be at my execution tomorrow.

Yoga for Protesters: A Field Guide

Required Equipment

- Yoga mat
- Yoga tights or other stretchy clothing
- Water bottle

Pose to Protest Inequality

Place your mats on treacherous, uneven ground. Balance on one foot (Tree pose, or, if you are adventurous, Warrior III). Struggle to keep your hips level. Remain on one foot until the imbalance causes you to crash to the ground. Perform this pose in groups, mats close together —note that when one person falls, others are taken down with them.

Pose to Protest Misogyny

Place your mats on the floor. Turn your back to the source of the misogynistic behavior. Bend forward, placing your palms on the mat, and step back into Downward-facing Dog. Arch your back and raise your hips to the sky. Do not smile, even if told you will look pretty doing so. If possible, fart in the direction of the misogynist.

Pose to Protest Vote Suppression

Place your mats as close to the polling location as allowed. (This ranges from 300 feet from the entrance in Iowa to 25 feet from the entrance in Missouri—be sure to check your state statutes.) From basic Mountain pose, step back with one foot and raise your arms to shoulder height (Warrior II). Imagine you are as long and as thin as a ballot envelope. Hold this position until you feel you have been counted.

Pose to Protest Unaffordable or Unobtainable Healthcare

Bring your mats to a healthcare facility and place them in an area where your class will not obstruct anyone seeking healthcare. Perform any sequence of standing poses and finish by laying supine on your mat in Corpse pose. Remain there for as long as you can afford to, and remember to keep breathing.

Pose to Protest Political Corruption

Place one mat in the hallway outside the politician's office. Take turns with other constituents using the mat for regular yoga practices. It is fine to do any version of Hatha, Iyengar, Vinyasa, or Ashtanga. Be careful of the slippery environment. When the politician is under investigation or indictment, you can switch to Bikram (hot) yoga for the duration.

Pose to Protest Mindboggling Stupidity

This is one of the easiest poses to maintain—which is fortunate, because it is the pose you will most often be inspired to use. It does not require a mat. Use it at the supermarket, at your child's school, at your parent's retirement community, at the Motor Vehicle Licensing Office, or in any bureaucratic environment. Simply step back with one foot into Warrior I, throwing your arms into the air, raising your face to the sky, rolling your eyes, and silently asking, "What. The. Fuck?" Your ability to maintain this pose will increase dramatically with practice. And you should have no problem finding reasons to practice for several minutes, every day.

The Last Call from Amelia Shea

I tugged open the sliding glass door at sunset and stood in the doorway, listening to the crash of waves on the jagged rocks down below. It would have been sweet to put a chair out on the narrow deck. But the Bauers had warned me that some of the planks and the railing were pretty iffy. The rotting deck needed work—so did the rest of the caretaker's cottage—but I wasn't complaining. Winter was coming; at least this year I'd have a place to stay.

Inhaling the scents of cedar and salt water, I thought about rolling out my worn yoga mat and doing a quick practice. Then my phone ran, shattering the mood. The caller ID showed: *Amelia Shea*.

I shoved the door closed and sank down at the kitchen table. My finger hovered over the screen. Accept? Decline? Amelia was an old friend, but the friendship had long ago soured. I answered. "Yeah?"

"Kate? Girlfriend? What are you doing tonight?" Amelia talked like I'd seen her just yesterday, her shrill voice rattling the battered smartphone. "I need you to spring me from this joint. Right now. These people are trying to kill me."

I smothered a sigh. Some things never changed, certainly not Amelia blowing things out of proportion. "Amelia, where are you these days?"

"In hell, girl. This is serious. I broke my ankle, they couldn't do a thing at the urgent care, they sent me to the hospital, and now I'm in this rehab place. Some rehab! The nurses are taking more drugs than the patients."

"Slow down." This was a pretty wild story, even for Amelia. "Listen, Amelia, I'm out on the peninsula. Housesitting a fancy estate for the winter. Can you maybe call an Uber to take you home?"

"Oh, honey! I left my wallet and phone at the urgent care and have to get over there to pick it up. Just come get me. We'll go back to my place. You can stay for the weekend. It'll be just like old times."

Old times? Yeah, those were the days. Thirty years ago Amelia would have been asking me to pick her up from some yacht club where she'd stormed off her latest boyfriend's boat. In those days, her paintings were in all the Seattle galleries. I'd taught martial arts and run a women's rights nonprofit.

But Amelia had long since faded from the art scene. And I'd just…faded. My social security wouldn't come close to paying for a place in Seattle these days. I'd gone from a studio apartment in the suburbs to a basement bedroom in a drafty Victorian to a one-room cabin in the woods. If the Bauers hadn't hired me to house-sit their fancy getaway, I'd have faced another winter in Tod's cabin, scrounging for firewood, shivering under a slimy camp shower, and relying on church food banks.

Amelia still had money, courtesy of a late husband who'd been a Microsoft millionaire. Now she rattled off the address of the rehab she wanted me to get her out of. "C'mon down, girl. I'm packed and waiting."

"But don't you need a doctor to sign you out?" That formality could mean shifting the whole crazy enterprise until morning. Or forgetting about it entirely. Anyway, I'd be off Amelia's carelessly baited hook.

"Ha!" Amelia screeched. "I'll take care of that. You just get your sweet little ass over here."

Well. It would be old Kate to the rescue, yet again. I grabbed a jean jacket and limped out to my Toyota Camry, hoping no cops would notice the busted headlamp and the dubious brakes. I found a station playing Americana and drove down to Seattle listening to Tom Petty, Bonnie Raitt, and Prince.

* * *

The nursing home was a squat, two-story building flanked by spindly rhododendrons. In the dark lobby, a halo of cold light marked the reception desk. Two healthcare aides, women, sat there.

"I'm here to visit Amelia Shea," I said.

The aides, fast food meals spread out on the desk, exchanged glances. The older one picked up a French fry and used it to point to a dim hallway. "Last room on the right."

"Thanks." I set out down the hall, wrinkling my nose. The low-ceilinged corridor stank of overcooked vegetables, urine, and worse. Through the half-closed door to Amelia's room, I saw an old woman hunched in a wheelchair. Amelia must have a roommate. "I'm sorry. I'm looking for Amelia Shea—"

"Girlfriend!" The woman in the wheelchair straightened up. She raised a claw-like hand in greeting.

I swallowed a gasp. The woman was Amelia. Her stiff hair was an improbable shade of red. Her face puffy, white as lard. How many years had it been since I'd seen Amelia?

"Let's go," she said. She swept a dozen orange pill bottles from her bedside table into a green plastic tote.

"I can't just wheel you out of here, Amelia. You need a doctor to sign—"

"Yes, you can," she said. "Tell 'em we're going to get some fresh air. Then you grab one of those crappy walkers they keep in the lobby. We'll leave the wheelchair, take the walker, and go!"

Amelia wheeled herself into the hallway and I took over, pushing her out to the lobby, listening as she loudly described the horrors of the rehab. Glancing over my shoulder, I spotted the doctor, a young man in a white coat, peering into Amelia's now-empty room.

"Excuse me, is that the doctor?" I asked the woman at the front desk.

She shook her head. "Nope. Doctor comes in tomorrow morning at 8." She grabbed another handful of fries.

"But..." I pointed down the hall to where the doctor had been. Of course, the hall was now empty.

"Kate! Let's go, girl!" Now Amelia was wheeling herself out the automatic doors to the parking lot. I followed her into the misty evening, helped her into the car, and then slipped back in to swipe a walker. Just as Amelia had promised, a fleet of them stood in corner of the lobby. The woman at reception ignored me as I picked out a new-ish one and trundled it out. We drove off, leaving the sagging wheelchair on the sidewalk.

"Head for my place," Amelia squawked as I pulled onto the main road. "We need a couple of Martinis. And I have Absolut, girlfriend."

* * *

Amelia's lakefront house in Seattle was on a winding boulevard lined with tall cedars. I'd been there—what, 15 years ago?—for a summer party. That was before her husband—Dustin? Devon?—had croaked on a Galapagos cruise. I remembered feeling utterly out of place with my long hair, batik jacket, and thrift shop espadrilles, listening as Amelia pointed out Bill Gates' compound on the other side of the lake. I'd left early.

Now the massive house was dark, save for dramatic landscape lighting at the entrance. I helped Amelia up the curved walkway. Forget the Martinis—it would be great just to collapse in one of her guest bedrooms.

In front of the tall double doors, Amelia let out a hoot. "Of course I don't have my keys. But not to worry. There's a spare under the third paver." She pointed. I dropped to my knees on the gravel path, dragged the paver to the side, and dug the key out of the dirt. I handed it to Amelia, who turned the lock and hobbled inside. She patted the wall, fumbled with a security system code, then flipped a switch. Light flooded the room.

"What the fuck?" she screamed. "What the *holy fuck*?"

The house was empty. The walls, once filled with Amelia's paintings, were bare.

"Call the police," she howled. "I've been robbed!"

I let out my breath in a hiss. Despite Amelia's words, this was no crime scene. The rooms were empty but immaculate. In the kitchen a ceramic bowl filled with fresh fruit gleamed beneath under-cabinet lighting. "Amelia, did you put your house up for sale?"

At the foot of her driveway I'd seen a blue-and-white For Sale sign from the most exclusive realty company in town. I'd assumed the sign was for the house next door. But now I wasn't sure. Could Amelia have moved, put her house up for sale—and forgotten?

"He ripped me off," Amelia muttered. "I'm calling my attorney. Gimme your phone."

"Who ripped you off?" It was nearly midnight. Nobody was calling an attorney.

"Jason, that's who. That little snake. I'll sue him witless."

"Who's Jason?"

Amelia's voice subsided. "My stepson. He wants me to sign papers saying he's my conservator. Not a chance in hell."

A stack of glossy business cards from a realtor sat on the hallway table. I slipped one into my pocket, thinking *This is so not going to end well*. And there was no way we were going to sleep here. We might be arrested as trespassers, since Amelia had no ID with her. Even now, a neighbor in this security-conscious enclave who'd seen the lights go on could be calling the police.

"We'll go back to my place," I sighed. We used the bathroom, turned off the lights, and fled. I got us onto the highway headed north. Amelia whined and grumbled about Jason this, Jason that, she was going to take care of Jason! for several miles, then subsided into a sulk.

Just past Lynnwood, Amelia spoke my name. "Kate?"

"What?"

"Thank you," she said. Her voice melted into a child's mumbling. "Thank you, thank you, thank you. I love you, girlfriend."

It cost me nothing, so I replied, "I love you too, Amelia."

Halfway to the Bauers' place I stopped for gas. A young fellow who'd pulled up behind us in a blue sports car walked over and asked if I needed help with the pump. I said no, and thanked him.

He hesitated. "Your friend OK?" He gestured to Amelia, slumped against the window, her hair a rumpled mop.

"She's just tired. Thanks for the help." I fumbled the hose back onto the fuel dispenser and we left.

* * *

It was past 1 a.m. when we reached the Bauers' place. As I helped Amelia toward my cottage a car came up the gravel drive behind us. *Damn.* Had the Bauers come up for the weekend? Just what I didn't need. Headlights shone in my face. I squinted.

Amelia grabbed my arm. Her nails were sharp. "Who's that?" she asked.

"No idea."

The car stopped and the headlights went off. It was a blue sports car—a lot like the one at the gas station. Sure enough, the young man who'd helped with the pump got out of the car. Had I left something behind? My debit card? How stupid of me.

"Oh, shit," Amelia gasped.

"It's just the man from the gas station," I said—and then remembered that Amelia hadn't seen him. As he came closer, I realized he also looked like the young doctor I'd glimpsed at the rehab.

Amelia clutched at my arm. "It's Jason!" she hissed.

I sighed. Enough with Jason, already.

"Hello?" I called out. "Can I—"

The man raised one arm. A flash, a bang, and Amelia pitched forward. Then the man came striding toward me. He was pointing a gun.

I tried to slam the cottage door to keep him out, but Amelia and her walker blocked it. I backed toward the living room, thanking the gods that the Bauer's crappy contractor had never put a light switch in the front hall. In the dark, I could hide. Or find a way out.

I ran into the kitchen, yanked open the sliding glass door to the deck, and stopped. I remembered the Bauers' warnings about the rotting deck. But what if the man *thought* I was out there? He'd run right past me and go out there himself...

Footsteps in the front hallway. *This was my only chance.* I backed away from the open door, squeezed between the refrigerator and the stove, crouched down, and waited.

First, his steps went into the bedroom. Then they came toward the kitchen. I clenched my teeth as he passed my hiding place. He stepped, one foot, then the other, out onto the narrow deck. A splintered board creaked under his weight.

Oh, please! I stared at his silhouette against the purple sky. And waited.

He turned his head left, and then right, and then left again, clearly puzzled not to find me out there.

If he comes back inside, he'll shoot me.

Then he put his free hand on the cedar railing and leaned way out over the edge, peering into the darkness. My heart rose to my throat. What if he realized there was nothing down below but rocks and water? I rose slowly and moved silently into the open doorway behind him. Calling on muscle memory, summoning every ounce of strength in my body, I aimed a front kick square to his back.

It connected.

He fell forward. The porch railing split with a crack. And he vanished.

His terrified howl stopped when he hit the jagged rocks. I heard a clatter of metal on rock that must have been his gun, followed by a splash. Then, silence.

I backed into the kitchen, grasped the counter, and gasped for breath. When the dizziness passed and I could breathe normally, I fumbled my phone from my jacket pocket and tapped 9-1-1.

"There's been a shooting," I told the operator. "At Marcus Bauer's place. Up at the end of Ten Pines Road."

I waited for the cops on the cottage steps, sitting beside a lifeless heap that had been Amelia Shea.

* * *

The next few days were a blur of phone calls and interviews. Marcus Bauer flew up from California. The insurance people came out. I kept my story simple: I'd picked up my friend in Seattle, we'd come out here for the weekend, and a strange man had followed us. He'd shot her, then gone out to the deck looking for me. He'd fallen to his death when the railing collapsed.

When the sheriff's deputy told me they'd identified the dead man as Jason Bonifaccio, the son of Amelia's late husband, I hid my recognition. I was all shock and astonishment. The condescending smile on the young deputy's face reassured me that he believed me. He thought old people were too stupid to lie.

* * *

I was out of trouble, but I was also out of a home. The consensus was that a frail 72-year-old woman wasn't the right fit for the caretaker job. Surely she'd be better off…somewhere else. So I packed up my stuff—there wasn't much left, really—and put it in the old Toyota. Driving in daylight, the broken headlamp didn't matter. I figured I could make it to Tod's cabin at Crescent Lake just in time to settle in for another miserable winter. The kiss-off money that Bauer had grudgingly given me would cover patching the cabin roof and installing a rudimentary shower.

It was late afternoon when I turned off the bumpy logging road into the familiar lakeside clearing. Sunset filtered through the giant firs, showing a heap of charred logs and boards—all that was left of Tod's cabin. Stunned, I stumbled out of the car and walked around the burnt debris, scuffing at the ashes with my hiking boots. I spotted my iron frying pan and a metal door hinge.

As dusk fell, the woods took on a stony silence. I sighed. It was time to find food. And some kind of shelter.

I drove into Aberdeen, picked up a bargain burger and a Coke, then drove a few blocks to the old factory district. I parked the car on a deserted side street where I ate, climbed into the back seat, and settled in for the night. I'd cracked the window just a bit so my breath wouldn't fog the glass and give me away—if the cops down here even gave a shit.

From under the seat I drew the handsome bottle of Absolut that I'd pinched from the Bauers' liquor cabinet. I splashed the vodka into my cup, rattled the ice to mix it with the dregs of Coke, and raised my drink toward the stars.

Farewell, Amelia Shea. What a life you lived! And what a life I'm living.

Leeli's Choice

Late afternoon light filtered through the towering pecan trees in our back yard and lit the cavernous room Jenn insists on referring to as my study. I sat at the desk, a monstrous dark wood thing her interior designer had picked out, and stared at my laptop. But my attention wasn't on the case file open on my screen. My attention was on the voices in the kitchen. My daughter's voice, soft and hesitant, and my wife's voice, as strident and peremptory as one of her campaign speeches.

I'd offered to go with her, but Leeli wanted to tell her mother herself. Now I could hear Leeli's voice tentatively offering the plan, then halting.

There was no answer from Jenn.

"Mom?" Leeli asked, her voice trembling.

More silence. Then the *clack, clack, clack* of high heels as Jenn crossed the tile floor. The splash of iced tea poured from a pitcher. The rattle of ice cubes stirred impatiently in a glass. The clank of a dirty spoon tossed into the stainless steel sink.

Then, finally, Jenn's voice. "You'll have the baby," she said. "End of discussion."

"But Mom, I don't *want* to have a kid! I'm in *high school*. I can drive up to Maryland and get an abortion. That's what people do now."

"*People*?" My wife's laugh was a mirthless squawk. "*People?* Well, that may be what 'people' do, but you aren't 'people.' You're the daughter of a candidate for governor of this state. A candidate who wrote this state's anti-abortion legislation. Do you realize that if you were to get an abortion—which you will not do—just the fact that you and I even *talked* about it could put both of us in prison?"

"Mom!" Leeli tried again. "Mom, get real. I am *not* going to have a kid. You don't even know this guy, he's not—"

"I don't care who he is." Here I could imagine Jenn giving that tight politician's smile she uses on TV when she doesn't like the interviewer's questions. "This boy and his parents are going to make nice for the cameras and you two are going to have a nice little wedding. Look, you can always get divorced after the kid is born. Divorce is legal in this state. Murdering babies is not."

Rage flooded through me. I stood up from the desk, the desk chair scraping the floor. The shotgun wedding scenario? Jenn knew it only too well—because she'd acted it out with me 18 years earlier. In a week's time I'd gone from packing a knapsack for a year of post-law-school travel around the world to standing at the altar with a woman I'd met at a friend's graduation party and had sex with once. And not very good sex, at that. One date with Jenn, one broken condom, and I'd been chained to her for life. Her father, a local judge, had seen to that.

When Leeli came to me about her unexpected pregnancy I knew immediately that I wanted spare her the same fate I'd suffered. I told her I'd take her up to Maryland for an abortion. My law partner's girlfriend had gone up there last summer. They knew an excellent clinic. I would have explained all this to Jenn, but Leeli was afraid that would trigger another one of our epic fights.

"But Mom," Leeli wailed as I strode toward the kitchen, "I'm only six or seven weeks pregnant. It's not a baby."

Oh no, I thought. *Wrong argument.*

Jenn launched into her campaign speech about baby killers. "You are carrying a life, a human being, and a little one who can hear—"

"Shut up," I said.

They both spun around. Leeli, perched on a stool at the granite counter. Jenn, hands on hips in the middle of the kitchen.

"Leeli made a mistake," I said in the calm, even tones I use when presenting a case in court. "She went to a party, had a few beers, and let a friend of Nate Jackson's drive her home. They ended up in the back seat of his car."

I took a few steps into the kitchen and put a hand on Leeli's shoulder. At my touch, she burst into tears, turning and burying her head in my shirt just the way she had when she was five and had fallen off the swing set. "I'm taking Leeli up to Maryland. I've made arrangements. The hell with your campaign, Jenn. This is our daughter. This is her *life*."

"It's the *baby's* life I'm concerned about, Derek," Jenn shot back.

"Spare me," I said. "It's your campaign you're worried about. Babies? They're just planks in your party's platform."

Jenn's eyes blazed. Her lips curled back from her teeth. For a second I thought she might report me to the police for planning an abortion and then publicly cast herself as the family martyr. But that tactic was too incredible, even for my publicity-crazed wife. Yet.

"Look," Jenn took a deep breath and spoke slowly. Her glass was now empty of tea, but she swirled it, rattling the ice cubes. "I'll make you two a deal. Leeli and this boy get married privately. Just so there's something on paper. She'll have the baby, and then there's a divorce. We'll pay all the expenses and help Leeli raise the kid. Problem solved."

"Mom, the guy—" Leeli hesitated. She looked up at me.

I gave her shoulder a squeeze and nodded, "Go ahead."

"The baby's father..." she said, and stopped again.

I looked hard at Jenn and finished Leeli's sentence. "The baby's father is Black."

Jenn's iced tea glass hit the floor and shattered. Ice cubes and sharp shards flew across the tile. She slammed her manicured hands flat on the counter, and lowered her head. "Fuck."

"So, how does that work with your plans?" I asked. "Is your party ready for a White governor with a Black grandchild?"

Jenn shook her freshly dyed auburn curls and raised her head. Her eyes gleamed with hate and anger. "OK. Fine. Go to up Maryland, you two. Just make goddamn sure that no one hears anything about it."

I felt my daughter's shoulders relax. The worst was over. We'd get to Maryland.

An ugly smile crept over Jenn's finely sculpted features. "When you two come back," she said. "You'll do anything I ask. Because if you don't, well, I'd just have to obey the law and turn both of you in." She whirled and clattered out of the kitchen, leaving the broken glass on the floor. "Unbelievable," she muttered as she crossed through the dining room.

It was unbelievable, all right.

Leeli, still sobbing, slid off the stool, took a broom from the closet, and began sweeping up the glass. I brought over the dustpan and held it as she swept.

"I'll finish the arrangements," I whispered. "I have a special cell phone and Uncle Pete is handling all the email. Just don't tell any of your friends." I let the broken glass slide off the dustpan and rattle into the trash.

"I won't," Leeli whispered back. "Shit. I wish I hadn't said anything to Mom."

I didn't answer, just gave her a hug before she headed upstairs to her room.

I went back to my study. The sun had set, and a chill breeze from the garden was pouring in through the open French doors. I closed them, sank into the desk chair, and reached for my laptop. I opened a password-protected file labeled Future. I read, once again, my carefully prepared petition for divorce from Jenn. Now, I knew, it would be many, many years before I dared file it. If ever.

* * *

It was early in the morning when Leeli and I started for Maryland, where we'd stay with my brother Pete and his wife, Lorraine. With any luck, the clinic would give Leeli the abortion pill—two pills, actually—and she'd spend the next few days recuperating in Pete's guest room.

"Been there, done that," Lorraine had said over the phone. "I'll take the best care of her."

Lorraine, a nurse, explained that it might take a few days to make sure the pills had worked completely. "So you can't take the chance of driving right back home, and then her needing to get more medicine or go to a hospital," she said. "People down your way are being sentenced to prison just for having miscarriages. If those folks think Leeli's had an abortion—well, never mind. She'll stay right here with us until we're absolutely sure that everything's fine."

We drove north along scenic back roads. I didn't tell Leeli I was trying to avoid leaving any evidence of our trip on highway security cameras. When we stopped for lunch at a drive-through burger place, I paid cash. There could be no traces of this trip. I was so wrapped up in figuring out security issues that we were halfway to Maryland before I registered Leeli's silence. She'd always been a quiet kid, but a cheerful one. Now, as we drove, she looked haunted. She'd barely nibbled at her hamburger.

"Dad?" she said.

"Sweetie?"

More silence.

"Dad, what if I changed my mind?"

I opened my mouth to tell her not to be ridiculous, but

fortunately stopped myself. "Well," I said, "You could do that. Tell me what you're thinking."

She shrugged, her shoulders bony and narrow in her white cotton t-shirt. She stared out the window at the lush green farmland as she spoke. "I...I think I want to keep the baby and raise them by myself. Or, at least, have the baby and then a family could adopt them."

"Wait. Did your mother try—"

She shook her head vigorously, then looked over at me. "No. Dad, this was my idea. I just...feel this way. I'm...sorry."

I felt ridiculous speeding along a winding country road to an appointment it now appeared we would not be keeping, staring at the road when I should be looking at my little girl. I spotted a fruit-and-vegetable stand up ahead, pulled into their gravel parking lot, and turned off the engine. There we were, surrounded by wheat. We rolled down the windows. The hot, humid air poured in, but along with it the sweet smells of the fields.

I was reluctant to look at Leeli, but when I turned to her, she gave me her wonderful, shy smile.

"Is this OK, Dad? I know that you've gone to so much trouble..."

"It's OK." Actually, it was very OK. I'd had nightmares imagining Leeli at the clinic. Now I realized I could easily envision her pregnant, having the baby, and giving it up to a good home. Or, keeping it. She'd be a good mother, though I couldn't imagine how she'd turned out that way, being raised by Jenn.

And, I realized with a jolt, with her new decision I'd regained my own dream. The one of finally getting free of Jenn. Of taking that backpacking trip around the world that I'd delayed for nearly 20 years.

I thought for a moment of telling Leeli about the circumstances of her own birth. But that was for some time much, much later. Or maybe never. This kid had plenty to handle already with the pregnancy, her mother's rabid political ambitions, and possibly the responsibilities of impending motherhood.

"So, you're OK with this, Dad?" Leeli asked. She picked up her milkshake and took a healthy sip, apparently confident of my reply.

I smiled. "Sweetie, this is completely your choice. All I want is for you to be able to make a choice."

She nodded.

So I texted Pete on the burner phone, telling him our plans had changed, to please cancel Leeli's appointment, and I'd explain later. I'd call him tonight and ask him to donate a substantial sum to the abortion clinic.

Then I started the car, turned around, and we headed back home. Leeli and I were silent as we drove, both of us imagining the future. The future that each of us had chosen.

The Second Term

"We're meeting with Pete and Marietta in 15 minutes," I reminded Gil.

He shrugged and passed me the ball. I jumped and sank the basket.

"Right here, Jason!" he called, loping to half court.

Reclaiming the ball, I passed it to Gil.

"Three points," he announced, and effortless made his shot. He flashed a quick grin, the one that had melted hearts when we were in high school and charmed voters on the campaign trail. "OK," he said. "Let's go give old Pete the bad news."

Gil headed for the elevator that would take him up to the White House executive residence, two Secret Service guys falling in behind him. As the lowly press secretary, I headed unaccompanied into the dressing room for White House guests and employees.

* * *

"I need you to reconsider, Gil." Pete Fosci, the chair of Democratic Party leaned back on the Oval Office couch, shaking his great leonine head. "You're the only one, *the only one*, the party has who can get the votes. We'd risk losing not just the White House, but possibly the Senate, if we had to start from scratch with a new candidate."

Fosci threw up his big hands to fend off our disagreement. "Sure, sure, it's gonna be a tight race. But your ratings are good, you're a known entity, and I think a lot of voters just assume you're in for that second term. Tell me you're in, son."

My boss, President Gil Perrault, sat in a chair opposite Fosci. Tall, slender, with a tanned face often described as "Kennedy-esque" he looked like a model for Louis Vuitton. Gil had his elbows on his knees and his hands clasped. He'd bowed his head, not in prayer but in exasperation. My heart went out to him. Gil had loved being the governor of the Southwestern state where the Perrault family had been in politics for generations. He'd never wanted to be the president of the United States.

"Pete, I'm not doing a second term," he said. "Marietta and I agreed"—he nodded to the statuesque Black woman who occupied the chair next to his—"that the vice presidency would be her springboard to the White House. She has every qualification. Far more than I did as a one-term governor."

Vice President Marietta Jones-Petit, a former air force general, national security advisor, and two-term senator from Ohio, had her perfectly glossed lips set in a straight line. She looked every inch the military expert trained to deal with the facts.

"Gil, I hate to say it, but I agree with Pete." Marietta gave a rueful smile. "As much as I want that job, this country is not ready for a woman president. Some of the polls say 'maybe.' But I've looked long and hard at the latest leadership studies. They say that say a significant percentage of men will still chose a man—of any race, and any party—rather than see a woman in a leadership position. Hillary Clinton couldn't pick up Obama's voters. The cold, hard facts are that I can't pick up yours. The election would be just too close."

"I disagree." Gil shook his head. "But if you don't want the nomination—" he looked over to me. "Jason, hand me that list, would you."

I passed over the list we'd prepared, and Gil regrouped. "Look," he said. "What about Mendez? Hugely popular governor. He'd do well in Florida and California, maybe even Texas. And Brecheen—he's got great support from the unions and the environmental folks."

Fosci and I exchanged looks. We'd have to let Gil talk himself out. He was still trying to sell Pete on Mendez and Brecheen when his wife, Kate, came into the office. She stopped and stood against the wall, arms crossed. Like Gil, she was model-perfect but her heart-shaped face showed worry.

Now I felt a twinge of nerves. Was Gil sick? Was it Kate, or their little boy, Aiden? Was there something Gil hadn't told us? Some sign that I'd missed?

As his basketball teammate in college and his press secretary since his gubernatorial run, I thought I knew just about everything there was to know about Gil Perrault. His interest in rock climbing (we now had a climbing wall in the White House gym). His love for Broadway shows. His passion for domestic issues, especially education and healthcare.

Now Gil exchanged glances with Kate, gave a sigh, and looked over at Fosci. His expression was almost defiant. "Pete," he said, "If I go along with this, I think you're going to regret it. The United States is going to have a woman as president someday. You're denying Marietta her chance and you're standing in the way of history."

"I'm sorry Gil. But I'm willing to be the bad guy to make sure you'll be the good president." Fosci's words were polite, but the tight smile, the confident shooting of his cuffs, showed his relief and triumph. His mission was accomplished. Gil Perrault would run for a second term. Gil Perrault would lead the party to a narrow victory in Congress. The party would have four more years to get its act together.

Fosci stood up and slapped Gil on the shoulder. "You're gonna win, son," he said.

A flinty gleam came into Gil's eyes. "I am," he said. "I'm going to win."

Marietta Jones-Petit, dedicated public servant that she was, signed on for a second run for VP.

* * *

The campaign was bitter. The Republicans and their media friends picked apart every speech Gil and Marietta had ever made, twisting their words and ripping them out of context. They even brought out an old scare tactic that played to the racists, claiming the fix was in: Gil was going to resign as soon as he won and—God forbid!—a *Black woman* would become president.

I'd been worried that Gil didn't have his heart in the race. But to my relief, he threw himself into the campaign. Gil gave some of the best, most passionate speeches of his career. Working with lawyers from the Voting Rights Project, Marietta rallied a network of volunteers to combat voter suppression.

To my personal delight—but my professional concern— Gil and Marietta took far more progressive stands than they had in the first campaign. They carried the flag for abortion rights, parental leave, and universal healthcare. Fosci was texting me during every speech, begging me to have them dial it down, until the polls showed the approach was working. In addition to pushing a progressive agenda, Gil was doing what Gil did best: Talking with Democrats, Republicans, and independents, and responding to their concerns.

"I'll be damned," Fosci said to me in late October at a windswept rally in Ohio. "Those two are going to nail it."

I nodded. We were listening to Ekon Petit-Jones, Marietta's husband, give a rousing address to a gathering of veterans. Ekon was getting quite a following of his own. Which was great, because there was something the matter with Kate Perrault. It crossed my mind more than once that Gil and Kate's marriage might be on the rocks. In campaign appearances, she came across nervous and vague. The press had noticed. I started to steer her out of the spotlight, using her mostly for photo ops.

As we got closer to Election Day, my job was to preserve appearances and make sure Gil Perrault looked like a winner.

Which, it turned out, he was.

Gil's inauguration was the victory party the Democrats dreamed of. Their relief at getting another four years to work on infrastructure—of the country, and the party— was palpable. Gil gave a great speech; the celebrations were exuberant. After the festivities, I took a week of vacation. When I returned, Gil called me into his office.

I passed Marietta in the hallway. Her eyebrows lifted when she saw me. "Something's going on," she said. "Sounds like you're going to hear about it first."

Gil's secretary opened the door to the Oval Office and then closed it behind me. Gil was standing at his desk.

"Have a seat, Jason." His handsome face was contorted in a frown. He picked up the desk phone and pressed speed dial. "We're ready," was all he said.

I was expecting Marietta to join us, but when the door opened, Kate slipped in. She closed the door soundlessly and met Gil at the sofa. They sat down across from me and looked at each other. But no one said anything. On the other side of the door, I could hear the aides talking.

I went into high alert. What was this about? Divorce? Illness? Wait—it had to be the resignation that Republican asshole had predicted. No wonder Marietta was quite literally waiting in the wings. *Shit*. The public reaction was going to be huge. I took a deep breath and looked at Gil.

"Jason," he said. "As my friend, and as my press person, you're going to be the first one to hear something that's not going to be easy for a lot of folks."

Gil looked at Kate, squeezed her hand, and turned back to me, smiling. To my relief, she was smiling, too. So how bad could this be? Gil was my friend. He was a great president. Whatever this was, I was going to make this work.

I leaned forward, nodding my encouragement.

"I'm coming out as a woman," Gil said. Another look at

Kate, who nodded. "I'm going to be who I've known I was all my life. I need you to—"

Kate interrupted. "Giselle, let's give Jason a moment."

I confess, I needed it. *Giselle?* My first instinct was to argue. Images of tall, lanky Gil Perrault playing basketball flashed through my mind. I knew Gil! He couldn't possibly...

And then I remembered Gil's words to Pete Fosci: *You're standing in the way of history. The United States is going to have a woman as president.*

And so we were.

I took a deep breath. What to say? What words to use? *Gil?* Wrong. *Giselle?* I opened my mouth to speak, then closed it. I wasn't ready.

The couple across from me were leaning together, as if for support, and watching me anxiously.

"Madam President," I said. As I spoke those words, a smile warmed my face. "Whatever you need. It's my honor."

Delia's Legacy

Clint Seeger spotted the three gravesites for sale on PlotsAreUs.biz. *Perfect*, he thought. The listing read:

> *Three adjoining plots in the Gracious Redeemer section at Magnolia Grove Memorial Park, just off Main Street in historic Sherville. Family-owned since 1944. An exclusive setting that has been sold out for many years. $10,000.*

Of course, Delia would need only one of the spaces, but he thought it best to have some insulation from other graves. At least for the time being. And, someday, if he weren't run out of town, Clint could be buried beside his beloved wife of 45 years.

* * *

When he received the Certificate of Ownership from

Magnolia Grove, Clint drove out to the old Sherville stone yard to order Delia's headstone.

"Sorry, Clint." Neville Parker, the Black man who owned the stone yard, shook his head. "You see, we don't do much in the way of headstones anymore. It's mostly boulders and pavers for those landscape designers down in Miami." He waved one arm in the direction of a huge granite boulder being loaded onto a flatbed truck. "I still do some engraving for family, but you'll get a much better price if you go with one of the big companies out of state. You pick a design from an online catalog and they ship your headstone direct to the cemetery. Sorry you drove out all this way. Should've called."

Clint listened, then shook his head. "Neville," he said, "This is a real special stone, and I need you to do it. Delia's ill, likely to go in the next few months. I promised her she could see the stone beforehand, make sure it's exactly what she wants."

"Sorry to hear about that," Parker said. He paused, sighed, and stepped one of his dusty work boots up on a slab of black marble. "Well, how about you folks write up what you want to see on the stone, and I'll get you an estimate. Artwork—you know, angels, trees, and such—those'll be extra."

"Money's not an issue," Clint said. "And we can skip the angels. I brought the inscription with me." He reached into his worn sports coat and drew out a folded sheet of white paper. "See what you think."

Parker took the paper, fished reading glasses from the pocket of his blue work shirt, and walked slowly over to the shade of the building. He unfolded the paper and read the few typed lines. Then he read it again. He looked up at Clint and raised a bushy eyebrow. "Just where you planning to put this stone, man?"

"Magnolia Grove Memorial Park. Gracious Redeemer section."

Both of Parker's eyebrows went up. "Heh. You don't say. Well, I can get you a real good price on this one. I'd say you're going to find out just how Gracious that Redeemer is."

The two shook hands and Clint strode back to his car. Behind him, he could hear the stone mason chuckling, "Magnolia Grove. Gracious Redeemer section. We'll see."

* * *

Delia died peacefully three months later—far more peacefully than she'd lived, Clint reflected. He received the usual round of effusive condolences that were *de rigueur* in a small Southern town. Many friends and neighbors, most of them elderly, attended the funeral. For all that Delia had rabble-roused her way through life, she and Clint were still from one of Magnolia Grove's oldest and most respected families. Their ancestors dated back to the bad old days of the American South. Especially as they'd grown older, their liberal opinions and progressive politics had been dismissed as quaint and harmless. One neighbor, seeing a "Biden for President" sign in their front yard, had told her minister that both of the Seegers had dementia.

After a quiet graveside ceremony, Delia Seegar was left to rest in peace for six months. Then, after the grave dirt had settled properly, her headstone arrived and was "placed" by the groundskeepers. All hell broke loose the following morning.

Clint was not surprised to get a call from Magnolia Grove.

"Mr. Seeger," the funeral director began.

Clint grinned. The man's tone, usually unctuous, was for once truly mournful. "Yes?" Clint said.

"Mr. Seeger, I'm afraid that your wife's headstone...well, it's in violation of the cemetery's regulations," the funeral director said.

"Really? You'll have to show me which ones. My attorney and I went over your regulations in detail, and he assured me my dear wife's headstone is entirely acceptable."

The funeral director began to splutter like a panful of fried green tomatoes. Meanwhile, reporters were knocking at Clint's front door. He hung up the phone and went to talk with them. He was prepared, with printouts about Delia's distinguished career in law, journalism, and politics ready in a stack by the front door.

Late that night, while everyone in town was busy watching the mayor trying to explain the headstone situation on the 11 o'clock news, Clint clipped a bouquet of white blossoms from Delia's favorite lilac bush. Then he strolled the ten blocks over to Magnolia Grove Memorial Park. The elaborate wrought iron gates of the cemetery were locked for the night, but Clint knew about a gap in the magnolia hedge out by the caretakers' shed. It was conveniently near the Gracious Redeemer section.

He strolled to Delia's grave, knelt, and blinked back his tears. "You're still giving them hell, dear," he said. "I love you."

He set the bouquet of lilacs down in front of a handsome granite headstone. It bore the epitaph:

Here lies Delia Jefferson Seeger
Lifelong activist, feminist, and crusader for human rights
Born Dec. 4, 1953
Died of embarrassment
Nov. 6, 2024
At the hands of the Republican Party

Unwanted Visitors

I'd closed the drapes against the winter chill. No snow yet, but the wind was shaking the fir trees and rattling the metal porch chairs I'd forgotten to bring in. Marie Hartunian and I stood in my bungalow kitchen cooking spaghetti, sipping the Merlot she'd brought and reminiscing about our days in grad school.

"I'm so glad you got back in touch, after all these years," I said. "Why, I realized I'm not even sure what you're doing these days."

Marie gave an odd laugh. Was something making her nervous?

"I think you'd be surprised," she said. "Maybe I can tell you the whole story over dinner."

When the loud knock came at the front door, my cat Shadow meowed and raced out of the kitchen.

"Lise, were you expecting someone?" Marie asked.

I shook my head. But by the time I'd set down the spoon I'd been using to stir the simmering sauce, I had a bad feeling. *Please don't let it be what I think it is.* In case it was, I snapped off the burner.

"Stay here," I said to Marie and hurried to answer the door. I knew the inspections we'd grown used to in Seattle weren't happening everywhere. At least not in the small college town where Marie lived.

I opened the front door. Two beefy young men with pale skin and close-cropped brown hair walked in from the porch without asking. They wore the olive-drab uniforms of the new Federal Security Agency.

"Lise Parker?" the taller one said, his thick finger poised over a data pad. His question was more of a statement.

I gave a short nod. "Yes."

"Routine check of the block." The agent's speech was devoid of inflection. He probably said that same phrase 50 times a day. Or, in the case of Federal Security, a night. They usually came at night.

His partner was already pawing through magazines on my coffee table, peering at books in my bookcases, and opening drawers in the table where I sort the mail. Marie had come out from the kitchen. Now she perched on the arm of a club chair, her open mouth proclaiming her disbelief.

I stood by the sofa, my eyes on anything but the agents. I always stood when Federal Security came.

The taller agent, the one who'd spoken, brushed past. I wrinkled my nose. His cloying body spray was an assault in and of itself. He jogged heavily upstairs to the bedrooms, squeezing his bulk through the narrow staircase. Meanwhile, in the dining room, his colleague stuck his hand in a vase.

I moved closer to Marie. "Security theater." I kept my voice low. "Ever since the new administration declared Seattle a terrorist haven—" I rolled my eyes to indicate the absurdity of it, "the feds have been sending these rent-a-cops around to keep us on our toes, keep us frightened. They'll check the computers, maybe ask to see my phone."

"But that's illegal!" Marie said, spluttering. "They need warrants! You should just tell them to leave."

I wished she'd keep her voice down. I kept my tone even. "Well, the feds have declared a state of emergency and they claim that means they don't need warrants. Of course, people are filing lawsuits. But in the meantime, putting up with these *visits* is easier than being arrested." I didn't add that my next-door neighbor who'd resisted an inspection had disappeared the following day. His bungalow now sat empty, the front lawn overgrown. The couple across the street had adopted his dogs. Had he left town? Or was he in a detention camp?

I studied the polished oak floor, listening as the agents stomped around the house. It seemed to take longer than usual tonight. When I looked up, Marie's dark eyes met mine.

She made no effort to conceal her indignation. "I guess I'd heard about this on the news, but that was months ago," she said. "I had no idea it was still going on."

So it was true, what I'd heard. About the social media companies filtering everyone's news feeds by region. People from Boston, San Francisco, Portland, and the four other cities the feds had labeled "terrorist havens" discovered that their social media posts about the FSA's inspections were never visible to friends in other cities. The only place you saw these home searches mentioned was on local discussion boards, where people complained that the gated lakeside communities where the wealthy lived seemed to be exempt from the visits. That politicians and city leaders, at least those from the right party, had been paid off to ensure that the city cops ignored citizen complaints about the FSA.

So many rumors. So hard to tell the truth from paranoia.

I didn't say this to Marie. We were both quiet, listening as cabinets opened and closed in my study. Then we heard the clacking of a computer keyboard.

"Don't they need your password?" she whispered.

"I, ah, don't use one anymore." Last month an agent had flown into a rage when I'd fumbled while typing my password for him. It was easier to just give them access. "It's only theater. If they really want to see what websites we were visiting, or what our emails say, they could just monitor the traffic from our internet providers. Maybe they do."

"Unbelievable." Marie shook her head slowly, her lips pressed together.

"I'm so sorry," I said. But what the hell was I apologizing for? Did she expect me to refuse the inspection and risk...whatever it was Federal Security did to people?

Footsteps came up the basement stairs. Cabinets opened and closed in the kitchen. They even opened the damn refrigerator. The taller agent came out of the kitchen and strode over to me.

"ID." He held out his hand.

I grabbed my purse from the hall table, rummaged for my passport, and handed it to him.

"If I'd known about all *this*, I wouldn't have come!" Marie spoke loudly. I wished she'd keep her mouth shut.

The agent turned to her, his pale, bland face darkening. "You. Do you live here?"

Oh, no! Well, now she'll see what it's like, I thought miserably.

"No," Marie said. She stood with her arms crossed over the front of her crisp white blouse, delicate gold bracelets dangling from her slim wrists. "I'm from Mondville. Where we don't have home invasions like this."

The agent put out his hand. She stared at it.

"ID," he barked.

Marie jumped. She slowly picked up her large leather purse from beside the chair, took out her wallet, and extracted her driver's license.

The agent read it. His expression soured. "Har-toon-i-yan?" He drawled her name with deliberate awkwardness. I'd forgotten that her late husband, Peter, had been from Turkey. Foreign. I hoped this wouldn't cause problems.

"Just what do you do for a living, Mrs. Hartunian?" the agent asked.

"I'm a science teacher. And my late husband was a tenured professor of civil engineering at Regional College in Mondville." Icicles dangled from Marie's words.

"And he died when?"

"Three years ago."

"Three years ago. So why didn't you just go back to your country?" The agent waited. Marie said nothing. The shorter inspector had emerged from the kitchen and stood behind her. I wondered if she realized he was there.

"Just where are you from, Mrs. Hartunian?" the agent persisted.

"I'm from Mondville. Born in Mondville." Her composure astonished me.

The two men exchanged looks and then the one behind Marie's chair glanced toward the kitchen. I followed his gaze. Then I smelled something burning.

"Oh my God." I pushed past the inspectors and ran into the kitchen. I was sure I'd turned off the heat under the saucepan. But somehow it was on High and the tomato sauce was spattering and smoking. I reached for the fan switch, but too late: the smoke alarm began blasting. I threw open the back door. I cursed as Shadow shot past me and out into the night. I grabbed a dish towel and flapped it until the smoke cleared and the alarm subsided. Then I ran back to the living room.

It was empty. The men were gone, but so was Marie.

"Marie?" I checked the bathroom and the guestroom at the back of the house. No sign of Marie. I remembered we hadn't yet brought her overnight bag in from her car. "Marie?" When I came back to the living room, I saw her purse had vanished from the chair. The hook by the front door, where she'd hung her blue raincoat, was empty. Had Marie left in disgust?

Or had Federal Security taken her?

Car doors slammed far down the street and I shivered. The agents weren't usually that loud. I turned off the living room lights, eased open the door a few inches, and peered through the crack. The shiny black FSA van sat a good way down the street, its windows dark, its headlights off. The passenger side door stood wide open.

The cold LED of a streetlamp revealed dark figures sprawled on the sidewalk. Neither one was moving. I gasped as it dawned on me that the two loud noises hadn't been car doors. Apparently they'd been gunshots.

At the far end of the block a car's brake lights glowed red. A subcompact car that looked just like Marie's pulled silently away from the curb. It drove slowly down the winding road and vanished around the corner. I thought about that large purse of Marie's. It had had plenty of room for a gun.

Then a movement across the street caught my eye. One of my neighbors was quietly closing their front door. Next door to them, curtains twitched in a darkened living room. My heart pounded.

As far as I knew, there were no government surveillance cameras on our tree-lined street. I didn't think anyone would call the police. No, they'd try desperately to pretend they'd heard and seen nothing. Could I pretend as well? Maybe. Maybe...

Just to be safe, I'd leave little Shadow outside tonight, leaving her food and water on the back deck. If they took me away tonight, a neighbor would take the cat.

I closed the front door, carefully, but couldn't help flinching as the deadbolt snicked into place. I looked around the living room at my books, at my paintings, at my grandfather's green mohair reading chair. I wondered if this was the last night I'd see them. I had no idea how bad things might be.

No one did, these days.

Acknowledgments

The following people were instrumental in the creation of this book and the stories in it:

My life partner, Tom Whitmore, who discusses ideas, puts up with crazy deadlines, and encourages me in every way and at every turn.

Bob Brown, the courageous founder of B Cubed Press, who has created a place for stories that are "too political."

The late Nina Renee Richardson, who read all my stories and whose friendship continually inspired me to write better, kinder, characters.

Debora Godfrey, my fellow B Cubed Press editor, who always knows how to make a story better.

The members of Sound of Paper: Kara Dalkey, Manny Frishberg, Laura Staley, Amy Thomson, and Edd Vick. Their incisive critiques helped shape many of these stories.

About the Author

K.G. Anderson is a technology journalist, online content developer, and author and editor of speculative fiction.

Her stories appear in magazines, anthologies, and podcasts including *More Alternative Truths*, *Welcome to Dystopia*, *Quaranzine*, *Galaxy's Edge*, *The Art of Being Human*, *Everyday Fiction*, *Space and Time Magazine*, *Metaphorosis*, *Factor Four Magazine*, and *The Overcast*.

A graduate of Yale College, the Columbia Journalism School, and the Viable Paradise and Taos Toolbox writing workshops, she worked at the *Hartford Courant*, Battelle, and Apple, and freelanced for the *Boston Globe*, Take Control Books, *January Magazine*, and the *Seattle Times*. She edits anthologies for B Cubed Press and is one of the organizers of the Two Hour Transport reading series. You can find her online at writerway.com/about

Publication Notes

"Patti 209" first appeared in *Alternative Truths*, edited by Phyllis Irene Radford and Bob Brown (B Cubed Press, 2017); "Everything Is Fixed Now" first appeared in *Welcome to Dystopia* edited by Gordon Van Gelder (OR Books, 2019); "The Right Man for the Job" first appeared in *More Alternative Truths*, edited by Lou J Berger, Rebecca McFarland Kyle, Phyllis Irene Radford, and Bob Brown (B Cubed Press, 2017); "Bad Memories, 2032" first appeared in *After the Orange*, edited by Manny Frishberg (B Cubed Press, 2018); "Unnoticed" first appeared in *Factor Four Magazine* in April 2019; "Wishbone" first appeared in *Infinite Lives: Short Tales of Longevity*, edited by Juliana Red (Third Flatiron, 2019); "Politics as Usual" first appeared in *Alternative Truths III: Endgame*, edited by Jess Faraday and Bob Brown (B Cubed Press, 2020); "The Bodies We Carry" first appeared in *Alternative Deathiness*, edited by Phyllis Irene Radford and Bob Brown (B Cubed Press, 2021); "A Sign of the Times" first appeared online in *Quaranzine*

(2021); "Yoga for Protesters: A Field Guide" first appeared in *The Protest Diaries*, edited by Vanessa Cozza (B Cubed Press, 2022); "The Last Call from Amelia Shea" first appeared online at The Last Girls Club (2022); "Leeli's Choice" first appeared in *Post-Roe Alternatives*, edited by Debora Godfrey, Phyllis Irene Radford, Lou J Berger, Tom Easton, K.G. Anderson, Marleen S. Barr, Ellen Killian, Rebecca McFarland Kyle, Manny Frishberg, and Bob Brown (B Cubed Press, 2022); "The Second Term" first appeared in *Madam President*, edited by Debora Godfrey (B Cubed Press, 2024); "Delia's Legacy" first appeared in *Southern Truths*, edited by K.G. Anderson and Bob Brown (B Cubed Press, 2024); "Unwanted Visitors" first appeared in *Alternative Liberties*, edited by Bob Brown, K.G. Anderson, Lou J Berger, Debora Godfrey, Phyllis Irene Radford, and Cliff Winning (B Cubed Press, 2025).

www.ingramcontent.com/pod-product-compliance
Lightning Source LLC
Chambersburg PA
CBHW020807310726
48969CB00002B/734